The Invention of Flight

Winner of

THE FLANNERY O'CONNOR AWARD

FOR SHORT FICTION

The Invention of Flight

Stories by Susan Neville

The University of Georgia Press
Athens

Copyright © 1984 by Susan Neville
Published by the University of Georgia Press
Athens, Georgia 30602

Set in Linotron 202 Baskerville
Printed in the United States of America

90 89 88 87 86 85 84   5 4 3 2

The paper in this book meets the guidelines for
permanence and durability of the Committee on
Production Guidelines for Book Longevity of the
Council on Library Resources.

Library of Congress Cataloging in Publication Data

Neville, Susan.
   The invention of flight.

   I. Title.
PS3564.E852515 1984   813'.54   83-24142
ISBN 0-8203-0706-8 (alk. paper)

The author and the publisher gratefully acknowledge
the following publications in which stories from
this collection first appeared: "Johnny Appleseed,"
Apalachee Quarterly, Pushcart Prize IV; "Banquet,"
"Rondo," *Ascent;* "Rain Forest," *Gallimaulfry;*
"Rapture," *Indiana Writes;* "Second Coming," *Pigiron;*
"The Beekeeper," *A Shout in the Street.*

FOR KEN

Contents

The Invention of Flight

The Beekeeper

Lorrine's house in mid-summer. Kitchen full of plastic bags filled with bleached towels, dampening. The hiss of the iron. The outside softened through the gray grid of screens. Her husband's father lying in the yard in a hammock drinking gin and tonics, an old salt feeling in the gentle rocking the roll of the ocean, surrounded by the blue air, a yellow glass beading on a wrought-iron table, arbors of purple clematis and a hedge of white hydrangeas. The town itself surrounded by green rippling corn, by sloping rolls of hay like praying horses.

"Lorrine, more gin." She puts down the iron, reaches up behind jars of tomatoes for a new bottle, and takes it out to him. The bottle is full but the seal is broken from the watering down, every two bottles really one, every two drinks really one, and then he falls asleep after a few sips and she pours the rest into the hedge and later, when he wakes up, he says, "The old sailor really tied one on, Reeny," and she says yes, the old sailor really tied one on. He takes the bottle from her, pours some into the glass, mixes it with tonic, says, "You're a blessing to an old man, Reeny," and lies back into the hammock, rearranges the pillow beneath his head. His lips move out to meet the glass. He takes a drink and then rests it on his stomach which is round but hard for a man his age. His face looks healthy, tanned. A sun-bleached mustache rests, a pale scar above his lip. But his legs are too white, shrunken, and it's with difficulty that he walks from his room at the back of the house in the morning to his hammock and the return trip at night.

He smiles and Lorrine tenses slightly, realizes too late that his real purpose for getting her out here is that he's full of conversation, and she knows that she will listen too long, barely able to follow it because of his age, because she has never been to any of the places that he talks about nor seen any of the things he has seen and because, even after years in this country, his accent is still thick. A week ago he had spent a half an hour saying tshashoo, tsha-shoo, tshashoo and she had thought he was talking about sneezes until she realized he wanted a certain kind of nut. "I dinna learn from books," he says, moving the glass in circles on his stomach. "I saw the fish born in river and go fifty miles away but ever year they come hop hop hop back to where they born." He pauses, then goes into a long story, something about Finland and ropes, then without transition starts a childhood story about Den-mark, about walking miles through snow to see the *Queen Mary,* about his father taking him to see their cow slaughtered for the meat, a bloodstained broom and oil drums the things he remembers. Lorrine asks polite questions, has never been able to figure out how not to do that or how to get away from the rambling comfortably. She remembers her husband before he died had been able to just sit back in his own chair, close his eyes, and nod as if he were listening, a transistor radio that his

father couldn't hear bulging in his shirt pocket like ciga-
rettes, broadcasting a game from St. Louis.

The phone rings and she moves toward the door,
says, "It's the phone, Papa," and he says, "I don wanna
be a preacher, I don wanna preach. But some day, fifty
years, they will be starving, the people starve. The fish,
they not as fat as they used to be." Lorrine nods, smiles,
opens the screen door, and shuts it behind her.

She picks up the phone, says, "No," and hangs up, an
irritation but she's thankful for it, hears him call, "Lorrine," and she goes to the door. "Who was it?" he says,
and he smiles at her, lifts his head from the pillow,
wants her to come back outside. "Wrong number,
Papa." She turns back into the kitchen, says, "I'll be out
later with some lunch." She takes a linen towel out of the
bag and presses the iron to it. She thinks of the old man
in the back yard, no relation to her really, not by blood
or even country, but so helpless and so many years left
in him. In June a cottonwood tree two blocks away had
made drifts of white seeds at the side of her house and
he had thought it a late snow, had asked her to bring
him a sweater with the temperature nearing ninety. But
he knows several languages, has fought in wars and seen
death, his life more important than hers surely. She
seldom goes to church, is not one to believe in a literal
interpretation of the Bible, but she does believe that
God is love, literally, or, to be more exact, that love is
God, or at least the evidence, and she is sure that she
feels some love for him and that keeps things in balance.
She picks up one of his cotton shirts. There is a large
spot on the front that did not come out in the wash. She
will let it dry completely and next winter she will wet it

again and put it out on the line and the freezing, some-how, will take away the stain. This is one of the things that she knows and forgets that she knows. She forgets these things, then remembers them at odd times, re-members that feeding ground glass or oyster shells to chickens will strengthen the eggs or that rusty nails in the ground will turn hydrangeas blue, forgets them and remembers them with surprise, with a feeling of this is me, this is what I know. She forgets these things because her thoughts are filled with sea stories, with the sound of the old man's voice which she hears all day and as she falls asleep until it seems sometimes that he has drawn the ocean around them and the yard is water, the corn-fields water, the heat bending the air is water and at night the trees sound like waves and her bed rocks.

The kitchen gets too warm and she opens a window and hears him begin to talk to her through the screen. She touches the warm towels in neat stacks and the shelf of cool blue canning jars. "In Jamaica," he says, "the banana drop the pits before it die. Then a little tree. I ask where this come from, they say the banana tree know it going to die." She irons a crease on a pair of faded pants. The hot iron on the fabric smells like salt.

At night he sits in the room where the television is, where Lorrine and her husband spent their evenings, and he turns on the picture but no sound. The picture he uses as the other half of a conversation. He sees a shark on the screen and says, "Sharks. Now you in my subject," and he begins a long story about a shark. There is a rope tied to Matt Dillon's saddle and he says, "Ropes. Everything ropes. Climb ropes to get on ship, rope nets, ropes all on the deck, sleep on a bed of ropes." Lorrine goes in and out of the room, gives him small glasses of cherry wine from Denmark, brings him corn chips, turns back the covers on his bed, amazed sometimes at how she had spent all of her life first outside of this town and then in it. Some nights she tries to bring up her own subjects, to have a conversation, and he does try to listen, but something she says always reminds him of something and he interrupts her excitedly and begins talking again and continues for hours. But some nights she loves the skin on his face, which is like paper or a fine soap. Some nights she loves the skin on his face and his resemblance to her husband and even some of his stories, and other nights she sits by herself in the dark in the living room, her legs covered with an afghan, the sound of his voice roaring like the inside of a shell.

When their Social Security checks come on the same day, he sends her to the store for honey. He puts thick spoonfuls of it on the yeast biscuits that she makes twice a week, lets it drip and coat his fingers like glass, leave sticky dark spots on his clothes. He smiles like a baby when he eats, purses his mouth like a kiss to blow away flies. She eats some of the honey herself, but it is too thin, not as thick and dark as the sourwood honey her grandfather's bees had made in North Carolina or even the clover honey her father's bees had made. (His hat was covered with a net that reached down to his waist, his pants tied tight around the ankles. In swarming season, if a queen would leave and take the rest of the bees, he could find the tree where they rested on a branch, hanging together as thick and dark and long as an

Amish beard, and he could cut off the branch and take the swarm back to a new hive and none of them would sting him. "Bees are the gentlest creatures," he would say. "They don't know anger.")

She sees that there is going to be an auction of the estate of a man that she knew had kept bees and she makes sure the old man has plenty of ice and that it's not going to rain and she calls up her friend Eva whose husband had just retired. Eva picks her up and they drive out to the country. They ride almost as high above the road in Eva's old Studebaker as if they're on a tractor. She looks at the soft faded cotton of her dress and of Eva's dress. There is a faint pleasant odor of bleach. "Do you remember back when flour sacks were printed with pretty designs, the dresses we had from them?" Eva nods, pulls some hair away from her glasses, says, "I'm glad to get away from the house," and Lorrine says, "So am I. It's so pretty today," and Eva says, "It is," and Lorrine thinks at last, a conversation.

Eva tells Lorrine about her husband, about his boredom at being retired, and how she tries to get him interested in things but he seems to be giving up, looks older each day. Lorrine tells Eva about the old man, his nonstop talking, and they both tell stories of aunts taking care of sick uncles, mothers watching after grandmothers, mothers dressing feebleminded children until one of them dies, heroines to both of them, greater than anything that happens in war, heroines to them but crazy too in some way, and Eva gets bold and says, "A perfectly strong woman giving up her life for a child that will never be any good, what's the sense in that?" Lorrine says, "You're right, what's the sense?" She asks if Eva remembers Jim Harmon, the friend of both their families when they were young, who had left his wife and children in the middle of the winter and never sent any money, all of them too sick with the flu to get to another farm to get help and one of the children close to death before a neighbor stopped by to get some eggs because her hen had stopped laying. And the mother had gotten well and taken care of the farm and the children, wearing herself out in later years, but there was no question of who was good there and who wasn't. Eva looks pious, says, "The good Lord made that hen stop laying." Lorrine doesn't say anything, has grown up in a town where people claim the Lord sells their house when they're ready to move, that He makes the shopkeepers downtown have a sale on their size on the exact day they go through a pair of shoes. Lorrine has never had much patience with that kind of thinking, always remembers someone down the street who has cancer, so why is God worrying about someone's picnic or a pair of shoes.

Eva pulls into the lane leading to the farm where the auction is being held. The house and outbuildings are a local oddity, painted a light green with parapets on the top trimmed in gold because the farmer's wife had been from some place in Eastern Europe or Asia, nobody knew where. There are already around two hundred people in the yard, women picking through tables of linens, glassware, kitchen equipment, Christmas decorations, cheap jewelry, all of it arranged in boxes by the auctioneer but already out of order as someone sees a box of things she'll bid on and something, a potholder or bracelet in a box next to it that she likes also and she transfers it to the box she wants, this going on up and down the tables. The men stand at the edges looking at rusted farm equipment, sitting in overstuffed living room chairs on the lawn, eating chili dogs and bologna sandwiches, drinking lemonade. It's like a fair and Lorrine and Eva are excited, now and then hold on to one another's hands like children. They see people they haven't seen in years; they finger quilts and talk about embroidered pillowcases and they feel younger. Eva sees some green depression glass and she decides right then to collect it. Lorrine stands by the bee equipment and feels uncomfortable when anyone else comes to look at it, as if they're looking through something that belongs to her already.

The first thing sold is a gun. One of the auctioneer's helpers stands on a table, dark hair slicked back and workshirt sleeves cut off at the shoulder and unbuttoned, strong chest and arms. He holds the gun above his head and the men group around him. Everything wood, the gun and furniture, has been polished with lemon oil. Lorrine watches the boy hold the gun, thinks that someday he will be dead, and she wonders where a crazy thought like that comes from; she won't think of her husband that way. It's impossible really that he isn't still alive, his cuffs filled with sawdust and arms dark with sticky resins from his work so that he always smelled of pine. The way he would unconsciously crook his arm like an usher at a wedding whenever she'd take it, like a schoolboy, the pleasure in that. But she won't allow herself to think of that, looks instead away from the men and at a pot of begonias on the porch, a stack of books on one side of the begonias, an old jewelry box on the other, empty no doubt or someone would have hidden it in the bottom of a box of fabric scraps and spoons.

The gun sells and the fishing tackle sells and the tables full of boxes. Eva gets her depression glass. Only one person bids halfheartedly against Lorrine for the bee equipment and she gets it for ten dollars—two hives, a veil, a smoker, gloves, and a book. Someone tells her where she can get some inexpensive bees and she is so pleased that she bids five dollars on the jewelry box that no one wants and gets that also. On the way home she is so content that she almost sleeps. The air is the color of apricots and the fields stop looking like the ocean. The earth becomes solid again. She runs her hand over the worn velvet of the jewelry box in her lap and something small falls out the bottom and onto her dress. She sees that it's a delicate pink cameo and she almost cries at the beauty of that, not of the cameo as much as the fact that it has been hidden and now it isn't, something this lovely. Eva pulls up in front of Lorrine's house and Lorrine asks her in but she says, "No, Bill probably misses me," and Lorrine says, "And Papa me," and Eva helps her get her hives from the backseat and carry them to the porch.

Lorrine leaves the equipment outside and takes the book inside, is greeted by the old man, who shuffles in from the kitchen and says, "Hello. Hello. You know a palm tree grow tall but you put it in a bucket, even outside, it only grow to six feet." She walks into the living room and sits on the sofa, opens her book, and begins trying to read. He follows her in and sits on a chair beside her. He reaches over to touch her knee and she looks at him and nods and he takes it as a sign that he can begin a story and again it's the sea and places she hasn't heard of after the lovely day with Eva and she feels something unfamiliar. She knows he's tired, if only from having to get inside by himself and the walk from the kitchen to the living room, something he seldom does. She knows that he's tired and that he's probably hungry, but she doesn't get up to fix dinner; she sits and reads the book, holding the edges of the book tightly. He talks and she reads and finally he looks at her and is puzzled. He gets up and moves slowly out of the room, his legs so thin. In a while he's back with two bowls of dry cereal and two spoons. He hands one to her and says, "The milk I forgot," and she says, "Thank you," and begins to eat the cereal as it is without offering to go and get milk. Again he is puzzled, but he eats it that way too, his mouth slightly open and crunching loudly.

He finishes eating and sits with the bowl resting on his knees. He plays at trying to balance the spoon on his middle finger. "I tell you about bees," he says. "The workers all female." She looks this up in the book and finds that yes, this is true. Her father had taught her how to care for the bees and gather the honey, how to find the old queen and replace her in the spring with a new one that would arrive in the mail in a small wooden box with a screen, but he had not told her much about the bees themselves, how they lived their lives. The old man turns in his chair to look out the window. The cereal bowl falls to the carpet, but he doesn't seem to notice. He begins a story about Jamaica, a family he lived with for a while when he was ill, the meals they served and the color of the ocean there, the design on the wallpaper in his room, the taste of breadfruit. *Queen bees,* she reads, *can lay eggs and hatch them without any fertilization. All the unfertilized eggs will be drones, male bees. The fertile ones become workers.* She looks up drones. *Their sole purpose in life is to mate with the queen. All of the drones leave the hive with the queen on her wedding flight. One of them mates with her and he dies. He is not killed by the queen, as is often thought, but he dies at the moment of intrusion due to the structure of his own body. The queen rips herself away from the dead drone and in the process takes part of his organs with her. She then is able to fertilize the eggs as well as lay them.* He runs his fingers along a slick pinkish scar on his arm. "Fishing," he says and leans his head back on the chair. "I want to fish." There is a picture in the book of fat drones gorged with honey lying on the ground outside the hive where they have been turned out to die. This happens in the fall or sometimes in mid-summer after the first honey flow between apple bloom and white clover. *He has no baskets on his legs in which to carry pollen and his tongue is so unsuited to the gathering of honey from flowers that he might starve to death in the midst of a clover field in full bloom.*

She puts the book down on the sofa and stands up, walks away from him and to the other window. The sky is clear and the sun just setting, the window glass filling with a deep blue. She looks over at him, his head still back, mumbling, needing to be bathed, to be fed. She feels giddy, is ashamed of what she feels. I could turn you out, she thinks, and my life would be mine. No more sea stories. The house would be quiet. She goes across the room to him and says, "He's dead, you know, he's nothing, not any place." And then she feels more frightened than she has ever felt before. She puts her arms around his neck, so fragile, and she says, "What kind of life is this, Papa?" and he puts his hand on her hair and says nothing.

Rondo

The wife of a pianist with hair to her waist leans too close to a candle and for an instant the spray of hair burns and glows like hot wires, filaments in glass. The pianist is sitting in the corner by another candle, in conversation with an androgynous cornet player who feels that she is in some way carrying on a secret though spiritual affair with the pianist right under his wife's eyes, because they are of course talking on a much higher plane than the pianist could ever hope to reach with his wife, who is much too pretty and too blatantly feminine to have any kind of intelligence. Neither of them notices the wife's burnt hair, and she runs outside the house, past the other musicians, and into the back yard. The cornet player sees her leave and feels triumphant, assuming it's jealousy, thinking kindly that it might help the wife to grow if she begins to face realities such as this, if she begins to stand on her own in the way that the cornet player has always had to do, choosing first the trombone and finally the cornet over the flute and violin, to the confusion and anger of her parents who were certain that instruments were extensions of the body, of the voice, and were created for specific sexes, but who were thankful at last that she hadn't chosen the cello, a woman's instrument that a lady would not play. This had been the first place where people listened to her, where they seemed not to notice the blue shadow of a beard on her chin, the thick shoulders and waist that she had begun to emphasize in defiance. At the end of the year she can go back home to her parents or she can go to New York and begin making the rounds. But she's afraid that she is not good enough. She leans toward the pianist, toward his words, desperately afraid of leaving.

The teacher, a composer and director, sits near the center of the room, drinking straight gin. He brushes a hardened crumb of cheese from his lapel, scans the room for a victim. He sees the flutist with yellow hair who is talking to a tuba man who has a wife and a new child and soft muscles in his stomach but who is no doubt thinking, as the teacher is thinking, only of the way the flutist's lips bloom on cold metal, cheekbones like soapstone. She is obviously uninterested in the tuba man and uninterested in the percussionist who comes over to join the two of them and begins to rub the back of her hair territorially, runs his hand down to the small of her back, the fingers of the tuba man's right hand tensing, swollen beefy lips tight. Most of the women and half of the men in the room are in love with the percussionist, and the teacher is for a moment worried, watches the flutist's eyes for signs of dilation, of interest, when she looks at him as he taps the stretched skin of her wrist, and, finding none, settles back. He knows that even though he hasn't written anything true in years they all hold him in awe, that that supports the illusion this is the only musical universe which exists, that the flutist will eventually make her way to him. He looks around at them, the students, knows that though they wouldn't admit it, didn't like to think about it, some of them know this is the only place they will ever have the courage to think of themselves as artists and that, too, the impossibility of the adjustment from being artists to being teachers or salesmen, hawking band instruments and uniforms at small high schools, will destroy some of them. At times he feels that he should discourage them, tell them they are no good—the good ones will only benefit from that. But he can't, says you are good, so good, possibly brilliant, and in turn they sit at his feet, they say it is only because of you that I am great, only through you that I am great, only with your greatness that my greatness grows.

The pianist has come to feel that conversations like this are somehow shallow, small talk about large things, has grown weary of them, would like to cultivate some distance from this, from all of it, the talk of techniques and composers, harmonies and forms, buildings filled with the cacophony of too many voices, too many instruments. Singers walking in the open, across a field, across a campus, still going over an alto part in Latin and singing aloud, not noticing or caring about the heads turning. The phrase from a Bach invention that follows him through the daily domestic things and at night will not, no matter how hard he tries, let him sleep. But the cornet player is obviously enraptured with him and he is kind so he continues talking to her though he feels nothing for her, not even pity, only a mild curiosity about what she will be fifteen years from now, older, in a place she is not accepted, of course a failure. He listens to her and looks around the room, envies the percussionist his ease with women, with the beautiful ones, his hand a moment ago resting on the flutist's back, and now he is slumped against the wall, the dark-haired singer taking a drag from his cigarette, light gathered and reflected from her bracelet, an earring, as she turns her head, the beautiful line of her forehead a cool that he can almost feel on his own lips, the touch of ivory on his hands, the way she looks at the percussionist now, brushes against the sleeve of his jacket, not accidentally. The pianist wonders what it is about him, how people, things, are drawn to the percussionist to be taken, subdued, some lack of something civilized in him, of domestication, a pull of something somewhat like death. He sighs, turns to the cornet player, and tries to think of something intellectual, says God would come, possibly, if we called Him by His name, Jehovah, Yahweh. Peter would turn if called Pedro, but not if called Boy. He sighs, leans into the rough fabric of the chair, looks at the singer, and thinks Janice, thinks Juanita, says the trouble is that some names are too sacred to be spoken.

The flutist sees that the teacher is watching the singer with the percussionist and, triumphant from having ignored the percussionist's touch, she leaves the tuba man in mid-sentence and goes over to sit on the floor in front of the teacher, to bring his gaze to her, secure in the knowledge that she is the one true genius, that her music is not derivative. She can feel the cool underside of the flute on her thumbs, the complication of the valves on her fingers. She purses her top lip and blows down-

ward, feels the warmth of the air on her chin. There is
music in that also. She knows that the teacher knows
this, is drawn to her because of it, that he in fact loves
her, sees her in his fantasies, slim and smooth as metal.
She has been his student for years, only lately has she
begun to demystify him, to realize that the abstraction,
the look of the composer, is cultivated, as his music
lately has become, neat formulas repeated from when
he was younger, the hair and the skin graying too fast.
He is prey to imaginary illnesses, sellers of vitamins and
magical yeasts, close to but not yet an old man and
afraid of it, fewer women each year. He is bear-like,
hoary, reaches out to touch her arm, the roundness of
it, tells her that she is quite beautiful, says let us invent
one another, and she feels her head bow, her arms slyly
and consciously rise toward him until they are level
with her face—elbows, wrists, fingertips touching as if
bound.

The singer knows that she is nothing to the percussionist and feels that that somehow protects her, this
awareness of his motives, the way he automatically
reaches for women like a newly blind man who, in order
to move from this room to the next, this street to the
next, constantly must feel the touch of something—a
chair, a wooden table, a railing, a bush, a tree—or be
overwhelmed by the immensity of space around him,
once teeming but now, without sight, empty. She realizes also that he is not indiscriminate, reaches only for
the beautiful, the talented, is flattered by this attention
at the same time she is aware of a certain danger in the
clearness of his eyes, the practiced fumbling with keys at

doorways, the lovely structure of his face and shoulders, his hands, something sinister in the way he expects always to be met with yes, with compliance, is so sure of this that he never asks. The one frightening truth she learned as a young girl is that men who ask if they can kiss her are the ones she never wants to kiss. As he talks she becomes aware of the texture of the black wool dress on her skin, the way it tapers to her wrist, the slimness of that, the heartbreaking beauty of the silver in her bracelet. She moves her hand to watch the light catch in the bracelet, to watch the grace of her own fingers, something she seldom notices, how good the air feels to her, the night. She can feel herself wanting to hum, to sing, imagines how she will look on her first album cover, a famous jazz singer performing for audiences of thousands, each one of them in love with her and she distant, remote. There are certain songs she hears which are so beautiful that she can't bear to think that she hadn't written them, certain voices so perfect that she can close her eyes and feel them in her throat. The percussionist touches her face and she knows the smoothness of her skin beneath the thumb that he runs in a half moon from her cheekbone to chin. He tells her that he's been in love with her for years, has worshiped her voice, that she is more talented than he, more intelligent than he, that he feels a kinship with her, something mystical, that he wants to be a part of her greatness, and she leans against the wall, catches her lower lip in a tooth, is aware of the movement, the roundness of her breasts, moves toward him finally at the same moment that his eyes grow cloudy, that he looks away, that he turns to leave.

In the kitchen, the percussionist has to step over the tuba player to get to the bottles on the counter. He fills his glass with straight bourbon, knows he is already drunk, can't remember exactly what he's said to the singer, but knows he could have her if he wanted, if that's what he wanted, is not sure. To take the risk of the rhythm being not right, the sound of springs becoming at one time more important to him than anything, he now sleeps only on a mattress, hoping still for perfect syncopation not a matter of technique but of communication like jazz artists who can improvise together, a rarity. And the women, paradoxically, thinking of him only as an object, building romantic fantasies about him, returning always to the others, the ones they take seriously so that now he gets rid of them before they have that chance. He slides down the kitchen counter, sits on the floor next to the tuba player who leans his red cheeks toward him and asks which one he's taking home, what's it like, is it true that it's awful the morning after. The percussionist pities the tuba player but doesn't answer him, takes a sip of his drink, thinks that the mornings are the best part. His mouth always tastes sweet when he wakes, no matter how much he's had to drink, and he always wakes before the woman so that he looks at her asleep in the light, more innocent, and he goes downstairs, makes coffee and toast, puts on music, and sits looking out a window. In the winter he makes a fire, never is reading the paper when she comes down in one of his bathrobes, hair combed by now, warmed by the mug of coffee he has for her, by the fact that he's been waiting for her, that he does in fact have respect for her. Then the civilized conversation about books, about music, and he never asks her to go, always lets her decide on the right time. He has never been disappointed. As he begins to get up from the floor, the tuba player says my wife thinks you're sexy, sometimes I think she pretends that I'm you, and the percussionist reaches a hand down to him, says come back and join the party, but the tuba player shakes his head, no, takes some of his drink, which is bright red from sweet cherry juice and which sickens the percussionist. He leaves the kitchen, having decided that the singer would be pleasant in the morning even if perhaps disappointing at night. He stops in the doorway, thinks that he's been to bed with half the women in the room, that they've told him their secrets, all comfortably now in conversation as if there isn't someone in the room who could suddenly shout I know you, I know who you are, what you're afraid of. He looks at them, the flutist, the singer, the rest of them, even the cornet player, the pianist, the teacher himself, decides that they're all hideously alike in some way, pauses, feels suddenly that the room is too small, too full, leaves through the side door and no one notices.

The back yard is circled by small trees, the base of the trunks wrapped in white tape like the legs of race horses. They make her feel wild like the dry brittle leaves she's sitting on and the wind and the movement of branches reflected in the at-night-black glass of the small greenhouse make her feel wild. She holds a leaf to the part of her face that feels hot from the flame. There is the pleasant odor of dust, of stems, a rusted scythe blood red among the weeds, the red of the quince bush, dried foliage of peonies and geraniums, she is mad for this, for all of it. She sees the drummer come out the door to the side yard. Always he has smiled at her, the kindest smile, and passed on. He doesn't see her now, sits down at the base of a tree, stretches one leg out in front of him, then the other, slowly, like an old man would. Somewhere there is the sound of hammering, the movement of birds, a boy practicing archery in a yellow lighted garage two houses down, a loose wire thudding rhythmically on a wooden house. She sees the drummer put his head back against the tree, look up, the strength of his hand running down his leg to one knee, knows that he is feeling the same things she is, hearing, seeing the same things, and she thinks of going to him, of saying something to him, but she doesn't. Instead she too leans back, looks up, stars tangled in the emptying branches of trees, of wires, and all of it, all of it singing.

Kentucky People

S ummer, and the sidewalk cracks are lush with weeds; the concrete buckles. Last year's crop of high school pom-pom girls push strollers with new babies over the waves of sidewalk, the wheels catching. A factory that makes car seat cushions sends out clouds of white fallout, coating flowers. A half acre of old tires catches fire and smoulders.

Mrs. D. watches through her screen. She knows the names of the girls' grandparents, remembers the factory strikes when executive wives kept guns in their cars next to their children. She was born in the corner house defined by the sidewalks, was almost blown out the upstairs window trying to save her good silk dress from the Walnut Street tornado. Fifty years ago she danced under the stars in an indigo dress at her senior prom and that night went to bed with TB until she rose a year later, cheerful and undaunted. She sees the girls and their strollers, but she doesn't see the white dust on the flowers and she's unaware of the burning tires. In the spring she hides plastic daffodils among last year's dried-up weeds. Before the factory, the streets were paved with star bricks and trod by pony carts, dress materials were fine and costly and one-of-a-kind, her house the cornerstone of the finest neighborhood. Her house is wood, painted white, very little of it chipping, and that in the back. An asbestos roof is lined with delicate lightning rods.

Energetic, still known for her cheerfulness, she looks twenty years younger than she is, even in bright sunlight. She attributes it to the Normans, Merle and Vincent Peale. Her husband looks older—gray, almost too thin—but he too suffers from a constant optimism which keeps his paper-dry skin healthily pink, his movements agile, his eyes clear. He has a small business and still works at age seventy. When anyone new moves into the neighborhood, they're the first ones to call with a loaf of sweet bread. They never had children, and they're the kind of long-married couple that other people point to and say, "How like newlyweds," or "Married couples stay more in love if they don't have children." They go out for dinner at least twice a week, have friends in at least once. They make charming dinner companions. Mr. D. brings his wife cinnamon toast and coffee on a tray every morning before she gets out of bed. In all their years of married life, no one has ever seen them disagree about anything, even though they both have strong opinions.

Mrs. D. hears a knock at her back door and turns back through her living room and out through the kitchen. A short, stubby woman in bermuda shorts stands with her back to the door, bent over and clapping for a dog to stay in the yard. "Mrs. Lovelace," Mrs. D. smiles. "Call me Lonnie," the woman says, then, "Just a minute" and she runs after the small dog, dragging it back and attaching it to a post by a two-foot chain. The post is in the sun and Mrs. Lovelace always forgets to leave water when she goes to work. Mrs. D. has mentioned it a hundred times and Mrs. Lovelace always seems to take it to heart, but she continues to forget the water and she never moves the post, so that Mrs. D. has decided that Mrs. Lovelace is probably feebleminded like many of the Kentucky people seem to be, as much as she hates to say it, using old television tubes for target practice, and hanging sheets at the windows, their children always dirty and running around in underwear, and their houses crumbling. She finally decided that the Lord had just given her an opportunity to do good works when Kentucky people moved into the double next to her house and left her with the responsibility of keeping the dog alive while the husband and wife were off making seat cushions and their one daughter at home, a fifteen-year-old girl who was already pregnant and big as a house without even making it to the pom-pom squad, sat upstairs eating Oreos and reading *True Confessions.*

"You know," Mrs. D. tries again, "you could get your husband to dig another hole for that post over there next to the redbud, and your dog would get more shade." Mrs. Lovelace comes back up the steps, her dry, over-permed hair sprayed hard, a brush roller in the bangs and a metal clip in the back for no discernible reason. Mrs. D. doesn't open the screen door, but talks to her through it. "That jerk," Mrs. Lovelace says, and she looks away from Mrs. D. The sun makes her face look sallow, and Mrs. D. notices that parts of her face are twitching. Mrs. D. looks at her watch and notices it is two hours past when Mrs. Lovelace ordinarily leaves for work. "Don't you work on Tuesdays now?" she asks, trying to distract Mrs. Lovelace from the crying that seems to be inevitable. But her face still twitches and finally, without looking, Mrs. Lovelace reaches up to open the door and Mrs. D. steps back into the kitchen as the woman enters and saying "I'm sorry, could I have some water?" sits down at the formica kitchen table that is covered with two sets of Mrs. D.'s crystal—the amber and the green, this being the day she had planned to give them a good dusting.

Mrs. Lovelace picks up one of the amber goblets and hands it to her, letting out a large sob at the same time so that Mrs. D. lunges for the glass which she's afraid will meet its irreplaceable end on the kitchen floor. She takes the glass over to the sink and reaches up into the cabinet for a plastic one which she fills with tap water. She gives it to the woman and then goes over to the coffee-maker to pour herself some coffee. She wishes her husband were here. Together, with their positive thinking and their collective wisdom, they've counseled a lot of poor souls, often transient people like this one who have followed the industrial revolution from Kentucky to Indiana and most of whom are now out in Texas. They've taken in three or four runaway children at different times and turned them from delinquents. "Just give them love and let them know they're responsible for their own happiness," she would say across cut-flower arrangements at dinner parties. Mrs. D. never heard of a woman giving birth to a defective baby without saying "She must have had too many drinks or smoked or taken drugs" or of a new case of cancer without tracing it to an earlier tragedy, improperly dealt with. Her own life has been flawless, her health, after the TB, perfect, and she believes she can take credit for that. A regular churchgoer, she's proud she gives the Lord so little trouble. She never asks for anything when she prays, aside from world peace and other things she has little control over, and she's sure that the amount of His time she frees up by causing so little trouble every day helps someone somewhere, the Kentuckians of this world who are always, it seems, so miserable.

She takes her cup of coffee over to the table and sits down across the crystal goblets from Mrs. Lovelace. As frustrated as she's been with that whole family, she's excited by the opportunity to help them. "Now, tell me what's wrong," she says, "Mrs. Lovelace."

Mrs. Lovelace reaches inside her blouse and pulls out a Kleenex from somewhere among a tangle of straps, then starts tearing it apart distractedly and sniffing. "It's that man," she says, and in between sniffing and periodic sobs tells Mrs. D. a long story about her husband's drinking problem, how he's beaten her for years, but never badly, and how finally yesterday when he came home and started beating her fifteen-year-old pregnant daughter by her first marriage so that the poor sensitive girl had moved out to stay with a friend and said she wouldn't be back until the husband was gone, Mrs. Lovelace had decided to kick him out and told him as much. "And he just laughed in my face," she says, and she rips the Kleenex further as Mrs. D. watches the fibers hit the air and settle on some of the green goblets. "I decided that if I stayed home from work and I got me someone to help, I could move all his belongings out of the house and change the locks and then he'll see who'll fix his supper and who won't."

Mrs. D. stands up and starts moving the glasses over

to the counter. The beatings don't shock her really, even incest, which in this case it occurs to her is probable, especially since the man is technically the child's adopted father and not her real father and so could probably convince himself, if not the daughter, that it was all right, and especially since Mrs. D. has never seen any boys the daughter's age over at that house—even that wouldn't shock her. That's the sort of mess people get themselves into, and now since this woman has asked for her help the only thing to do is to decide on the right course of action and follow it. She turns back to the table and finds out from Mrs. Lovelace how long the beatings have been going on, how severe they were, all the time shaking her head at the nerve, the cold-heartedness of the man until she finally decides that yes, Mrs. Lovelace is right, he can't live there any more. "You do have to think of your daughter, Mrs. Lovelace," and Mrs. Lovelace, affecting a martyred look says, "Yes, my daughter."

Mrs. D. pours some coffee for her, fixes her a slice of buttered bread, and says, "I'll go change and then we'll start moving," and she leaves the kitchen and goes upstairs. She puts on an old house dress and tennis shoes and looks at herself in the mirror, thinking as she does so that she's never looked better. Her hair is still naturally dark, her makeup perfect, her eyes as lively as when she was younger. Nothing bad, nothing really out of the way, has ever happened to her. She shivers with excitement, runs her hands down her arms, smoothes her dress. You never know what a day will bring, she thinks, and she runs downstairs like a girl.

"Let's go," she says to Mrs. Lovelace, taking charge,

and the woman, grateful, gets up from the table, her face red and splotchy, the brush roller hanging precariously. They go across the back yards and up the back stairs into the house. Mr. Lovelace's clothes are already in a pile on the living room floor. Mrs. D. picks up a stack of things on hangers, Mrs. Lovelace picks up a drawer full of underwear and a pair of shoes, and they take them out through the front door onto the porch and dump them on a swing. They go back in and get the rest of the clothes in one more trip. All the while Mrs. Lovelace's tongue has loosened. In her own home, she seems particularly superstitious. "Mind you don't spill that salt," she says each time Mrs. D. passes through the kitchen. "Oh, I spill whole canisters of the stuff," Mrs. D. says, but Mrs. Lovelace acts like she doesn't hear. "Do you have any masking tape?" Mrs. D. yells out to Mrs. Lovelace, who is in the bedroom pulling out a quilt that was Mr. Lovelace's great-grandmother's, and dragging it to the door. It has become obvious to Mrs. D. that everything in the house that has any connection to the woman's husband at all, including wedding presents from his side of the family, are going out on the porch. "I want to be generous," she says, "don't want to argue about it later."

Mrs. Lovelace looks in her sewing box and brings out a roll of tape. "Just put a piece on things in the living room you want moved out," Mrs. D. says, "so I don't have to keep asking you; it'll be quicker that way." Mrs. Lovelace says that's something she would never have thought of in a million years, and she falls to it with relish, putting bits of tape on half the furniture and knickknacks in the living room. "That'll get me started," Mrs. D. says, and she asks the woman to help her with an old rolltop desk that's too heavy for her to get by herself and then she helps Mrs. Lovelace with an overstuffed chair from the bedroom and then they both take out smaller chairs and little wooden figurines and whiskey bottles they find hidden and old pipes and belt buckles, and one or two books. When they finally get all his things moved out, Mrs. D. looks back around the house and realizes that half the objects left scattered around the rooms are either crocheted or made of nylon net, including a giant nylon net chicken in the kitchen that's filled with soap. "It looks more the way I like it now anyway," Mrs. Lovelace says, "without his stuff."

The locksmith comes and changes the front and back door locks, and the two women go out onto the front porch, Mrs. Lovelace locking the front door behind them. Looking around them, they giggle like children. "Well," Mrs. D. says, still laughing, "I guess I'd better go on home." She wipes her hands on her skirt and walks down the front steps, then looks back at Mrs. Lovelace, who has stopped laughing and is looking at her husband's things. "What are you going to do now?" Mrs. D. asks her, and watches Mrs. Lovelace pull the clip out of the back of her hair and the roller out of the front and put them in her apron pocket. "Well, come on then," Mrs. D. says aloud, "we'll watch from my house," and Mrs. Lovelace gratefully follows her home.

"We can watch from in here," Mrs. D. says, and she leads Mrs. Lovelace out to her living room. Mrs. Lovelace sits down and bounces in Mrs. D.'s good needlepoint chair. Mrs. D. feels more energetic than she has in months and, leaving Mrs. Lovelace in the living room slumped down and pale, she moves quickly through her house straightening, getting things right. Each room pleases her; she's spent much of her adult life making this house. Not a single out-of-place object, not a single knickknack or chair that doesn't fit in with the color scheme or style of a room, and the color of one room fades thoughtfully into the next—her aqua living room, the light green dining room, the pale yellow kitchen. Only one crocheted anything in the whole house, a placemat she bought in Europe from a street vendor, and she doesn't own a scrap of nylon net. A corner of the basement is packed with things she has bought out of duty at church bazaars or been given as gifts—hideous plastic flower arrangements and macaroni paintings as well as nice figurines and vases, things that just will not fit in no matter where she puts them. She thinks that maybe she will tell Mrs. Lovelace to go down there, to help herself.

In the kitchen, Mrs. D. washes the crystal and puts it away. She comes back through the dining room and dusts a set of ornamental plates her grandmother had painted. She feels ecstatic; every once in a while she goes to the window by Mrs. Lovelace and looks out, but the things are still there, the husband hasn't come. Now and then Mrs. Lovelace breaks out of her lethargy to ask Mrs. D. a question: "How many sets of dishes you got?" she asks when she sees her dusting the plates and learns that they're never used. "Five," Mrs. D. says, "no, six, including the painted. Four sets of china and two everyday." Mrs. Lovelace is impressed. "I've always loved china," Mrs. D. says, "and so my husband every once in a while surprises me with a new pattern."

"How long you lived here?" Mrs. Lovelace asks a half an hour later, and Mrs. D. says, "All my life. I was born in this house," and she tells Mrs. Lovelace what parts of the house were added on, what parts have always been there, and what she and her husband have done to improve the property. Mrs. Lovelace asks her didn't she ever want children and Mrs. D. tells her that the good Lord didn't see to bless them with children and it wasn't her place to question that. "Instead of children," she says, "He made every day with my husband like a honeymoon." Mrs. Lovelace, bored, turns back to the window. "Of course," Mrs. D. says, "you have to work at it."

Mrs. D. feels generous and she tells Mrs. Lovelace about the pile of things in the basement and then tells her that she has to go to the service station to get a new right rear tire for her car; she'd promised her husband that morning that she'd do it today. "Is it busted?" Mrs. Lovelace asks. "Just worn," Mrs. D. says. She goes upstairs to change, comes back down and sees Mrs. Lovelace into the basement, picks up her purse, and heads out the back door to the garage. She sees Mrs. Lovelace's dog lying hot and breathing heavily, no water in sight, and thinks my God, I forgot about you, and runs back inside and in her hurry picks up a bowl from her every-day dishes and fills it with water to take out to the dog who drinks it and licks her hand. It's a tiny dog, female, and it's started into heat; already enormous male german shepherds and labradors are starting to loiter around the edges of Mrs. Lovelace's yard. "Something else to worry about," Mrs. D. thinks, and she gets into her car and drives out the driveway, bouncing as she passes over the uneven sidewalk.

She hurries because she doesn't want to miss seeing Mr. Lovelace. It's possible that he might make a scene, be so distraught that he'll throw a tantrum or he'll sit down on the steps and cry, and she will have to go out and talk to him, make him see the rationality of his moving, tell him how if he looks at the whole thing in a more positive way, he'll see it's for the best, that this may be the catalyst he needs to get over his drinking problem, that someday he'll be grateful that this happened. She sees herself talking to him, her slight figure reasoning with the tall, muscular Mr. Lovelace, almost handsome in some lights, but insolent, the way he lounges around the back yard outside her kitchen window all weekend, drinking beer with his friends, their laughing and talking that sometimes keeps her and Mr. D. awake on Saturday nights, the sound of car engines and motorcycles at two in the morning, all of them needing mufflers, all of the tires low on air and squealing. As she thinks about it, she can feel the excitement get stronger in her chest and her throat, the same place she feels the rare need to cry. Her eyes in the rearview mirror are animated, and she has to admit it, attractive for her age, maybe even beautiful.

She talks cheerfully with the couple that run the service station, sits inside with a cup of machine coffee talking with the wife while the husband puts her car up on a lift to change the tire. The wife goes outside to pump some gas and Mrs. D. sips the coffee, watches the wife through her own reflection in the window, now and then holds the paper cup with both hands to warm them, now and then runs the rim of the cup over her lower lip. A rusty pickup truck pulls into the station and

three scruffily dressed men get out the back, and while
the driver goes over to talk to the woman pumping gas,
the other three men come into the office and walk
around restlessly, picking up cans of oil and candy bars
and pens on the desk, and putting them down. One of
the three goes out to the garage to talk to the husband.
Mrs. D. deliberately looks out the window and doesn't
acknowledge them. For some reason the tension in her
throat turns without any change in the way it feels from
euphoria to fear. A robbery, she thinks. She's sure of it.
The other two men will keep the couple occupied, and
these two open the cash register and probably take her
hostage.

The men talk to each other. Construction workers,
they've been out all day working on a pipe. Their hands
are filthy, their faces and necks embedded with dirt. She
looks down at her own clean hands holding the cup.
Outside, it's clouding over for a storm. If I'm to be
killed, she thinks, at least it could be sunny. As if he can
read her mind, the wildest-looking of the two pulls a
gun out of his shirt. He holds it up to the light and looks
at it, a crazy smile on his face. The other man smiles just
as hard. He points the gun at Mrs. D. "See this?" he says,
and he shoots it into the wastebasket. "Air gun." He
shoots it out the open door, and into the wastebasket
two more times. He brings it over close to her, looks her
in the eye. One of his eyes looks at her straight, the
other points to the opposite wall; he smells like soil.
"Beauty, aint it?" he says. "I use it to kill squirrels." He
walks back to the wastebasket and fires it once more.
"Bet you could kill somebody with this if you got up real
close," he says to his friend. The third man, who had

been out in the garage, comes in, and the three of them get into a discussion about whether you could in fact kill someone or not. The driver comes in from outside and makes a phone call. The crazy man shoots his gun into the wastebasket again and Mrs. D. jumps up, spilling the coffee on her dress, sure she's going to be shot in the back as she runs out to the garage but too terrified to sit and wait for him to shoot her at his leisure.

"That man has a gun," she whispers to the mechanic. "He's shooting it," and the mechanic just smiles and says, "Oh them, they're harmless. They come in here all the time," and Mrs. D. feels like she's going to cry or make some kind of a scene, she's so incensed that the couple would let people like that hang around their station and incensed that the man would smile at her, actually almost laugh instead of allowing her the dignity of her fear, which was real and what any sane person would have felt when confronted with a crazy person, probably a Kentuckian, shooting a gun, even an air gun, into a wastebasket—a gun that a second before had been pointed at her face. "Is my car done?" she asks, furious, as she watches the man put the hubcap back on. "Yes," he says and lowers the car from the lift, still smiling at her.

She pays him out in the garage instead of in the office, gets in her car with the doors locked while she waits for him to go in for her receipt, and when she gets it, she backs out as quickly as she can, her hands shaking on the wheel. She can't understand what makes people behave like that, why anyone, when given a choice, would choose to be uncivilized. When she gets home she runs past the dog, who is out of water again, shoos away a graying golden retriever, and goes to the living room sofa and sits down, closing her eyes. She forgets for a minute about Mrs. Lovelace until she hears her coming up the basement steps with an armload of the most hideous church bazaar rejects. "I hope you don't mind," she says. "A couple of things were so pretty, I just knew you'd like to have them out." Mrs. D. looks around and sees, in the living room alone, at least ten different objects crammed into places where they don't fit. Mammoth candlestick holders with ceramic dolphins and giant ashtrays carved out of rocks and all of a sudden her living room looks more like Mrs. Lovelace's living room than her own. It's beginning to thunder. "Gonna storm," Mrs. Lovelace says, needlessly. "When we was kids, Mommy used to put us all on a big old feather bed whenever there was lightning. She said it would keep us from getting hurt."

Mrs. D. starts to say something but is interrupted by Mrs. Lovelace squealing and running over to the window. "It's him," she says. "The bastard's home." Mrs. D. jumps up and stands behind her. Again, the same feeling in her chest. This time she refuses to interpret it. She wonders how he'll act, prepares herself for the confrontation. They watch him get out of his pickup. He looks tired from working, his jacket slung over his shoulder. He pushes his hair away from his eyes. There are sheer glass curtains hanging in the window and Mrs. Lovelace, impatient with watching through a film of fabric, pushes them aside a few inches. He walks toward the porch, with his head down. It isn't until he has his foot on the first step that he looks up and sees his things. For a second he looks puzzled. Now, Mrs. D. thinks, now. Mrs. Lovelace pushes the curtain aside another inch or two, her hand shaking. Mr. Lovelace reaches down to get a handful of clothes and a pair of shoes, and he takes them out to the truck. When he comes back up to the porch, he's smiling.

In less than an hour he has everything but the rolltop desk moved into the truck. The last thing he takes from the porch is a box of toilet articles and a large hat. He looks over at the window where the women are hiding and, holding the hat in his hand, makes a large sweeping bow, still smiling. Mrs. Lovelace laughs and waves and then looks like she's going to cry. Mrs. D. steps back into the living room, horrified. Mr. Lovelace gets into his truck and drives off, tires squealing. "He'll be back tomorrow for the desk, I reckon," Mrs. Lovelace says. "He'll need someone to help him lift it into the truck." She thanks Mrs. D. and, taking a boxload of things she's gleaned from the basement, starts to leave. "Wait," Mrs. D. says, and she runs around the living room picking up the ashtrays, the candlesticks, the knickknacks that Mrs. Lovelace had placed there. "I want you to have these too," she says, and she adds a couple of things she had always thought looked right before but which she decides now will never do. She wants the room to look clean, streamlined. She picks up more things and puts them in Mrs. Lovelace's box. She wonders if her house looks like an old woman's house. "Now," she says, "that's enough," and Mrs. Lovelace leaves through the back door.

The sky gets black and a hard rain begins. Mrs. D. wanders around her house. At another double two doors down, the porch, slanting from lack of repair, is covered with half-naked children. The grill of an old truck in their driveway is covered with long strands of onions to dry. She looks out the kitchen window at the dog, shivering, but at least the other dogs are staying away, and she has water. Looking over at the Lovelace porch, she sees the desk is getting wet. When Mr. D. comes home, she's in the kitchen cutting apart a plastic trash bag. Ignoring him, she runs outside in the rain without an umbrella or rainhat for the first time in her life and she goes over to the Lovelace porch and covers the desk with the plastic. On the way back she lets the dog loose from the post. The dog runs around the house and under the front porch. Mrs. D. runs back into her own kitchen right after a loud crash of thunder, the whole back yard lighting up. "What's gotten into you?" Mr. D. asks, and for the first time in her married life she snaps at him in real anger. More loud thunder and she remembers stories her grandmother told her of lightning concentrating in balls and rolling right through houses. She runs into the living room, Mr. D. following her, her dress soaked. A flash of lightning she's sure is in the middle of the room, not outside, and she runs upstairs and grabs two feather pillows off the bed. The smiles of the men in the service station, of Mr. Lovelace. On the way down the stairs she meets her husband, who grabs onto her arms and shakes her. Across the dark of the stairway she hands him a feather pillow, hands it to her dear sweet husband, and says, "Just hold this, please, it might keep us safe."

Second Coming

At all moments I expect you. There are of course logistical problems. I know that you are hundreds, maybe thousands, of miles away, that you are not even sure where I am, but I decide that you are on the road and passing my exit on the interstate at all moments of the day. I imagine your call from the highway, calculate the time it would take you to get to my house from the directions I give, if I could get my face washed, clothes changed if necessary into something that looks less like I've been waiting for you, wonder if I should ask over the phone if you would like coffee or if I should use that question to get past the first few uncomfortable minutes when you are in fact here. At night, since you couldn't come to my house, I prepare excuses for each hour—who the voice was on the phone, why I have to leave suddenly for the truck stop, the store, a friend's, things I never do. The reasons must be more urgent in proportion to the lateness of the hour and there is a point when, even though I expect your call, I hope it won't come, a point at which my imagination falters, when all I can think of to say is it's him, I've been expecting him, or else I must say to you I'm sorry, I can't come, try again on your next trip through, knowing fully that this is the only chance. Both of these possibilities are unthinkable and so there is, as I say, a point at which I hope the call won't come.

My youngest is eighteen months now. Finally I don't need to keep my eye on her constantly. She can take baths with the oldest, and I can stay in the kitchen, make sure the dishes are washed and the crumbs cleared for your visit; I can do this without too much fear of their drowning. I try to keep their toys in one room so that you won't trip over them, so that my house won't look the way we always said our houses would never look— baby furniture in the living room, rattles, games, minia- ture trucks, and dolls in every corner. I try to keep them in one room, but most days it's a losing battle and on those days, if you called, I would take the children to a neighbor's, meet you at McDonald's, at a diner, take the chance that one of the women from church, from my club, might see me, almost hoping one might. Maybe you will come on a day like that. Of course you don't know, do you, that I have any children at all? You don't know their names or what they're like or what my hus- band's like (leaving each morning in a three-piece suit, carrying an umbrella, handsome, such a family man that women would never even try to tempt him, the dinners when we can't speak over the din of the chil- dren until we've somehow forgotten how to speak, eve- nings of paying bills, playing children's games, the moments, infrequent, when he looks at me and doesn't ask did you will this or did I?). You don't know that there is another child due in December, that I am already enormous from it. And you don't know how I was for those few years before I began to expect you, the way I dressed each day in a stained T-shirt, no bra, my grand-

father's cardigan, sloppy pants, white socks. The difficulty I had getting up in the morning, days spent with
the only voices children's voices.

I don't expect you've changed. The lack of concern
about the way you dressed became you, was somehow
masculine—the hole in the knee of your jeans, the
shirts you'd get at Christmas and wear the whole year,
no matter what the style—the plaid ones, the fancy silk
one with the French cuffs that you wore to chemistry lab
stapled at the wrists, the funny shirt covered with horses
that your sister sent you. You may have grown a beard
by now—that's the way I picture you, with a beard, un-
married, some secret source of income so that you never
wear a suit or sit in an office. The income is of course
necessary because when you come, when you're finally
here, you will simply take me to wherever you're going
next. You will have money and I won't have to worry
that I have no change of clothes, no creams or lotions,
no toothbrush. We'll buy the important things in the
next town and along the way you'll buy me things, all
the while telling me, as you used to, how beautiful I am,
how you like the way I touch you. I expect that you are
as attractive to women as you used to be, that you might
be with one tonight, but that you still are drawn to me,
almost mystically, that you are leaving her at this moment and moving toward me, will be calling in the next
hour, the next day.

Then there are days I think that you are already here,
that you're outside the house, timid about ringing the
bell. Those are glorious days, the days when I think
that. I reach down to pick up a toy and there is, I know,
grace in the movement. I look in the mirror and smile at

myself, touch my hair, certain that you are watching. At night I try to get my husband to dance in the kitchen. I laugh at anything he says, know this makes me look younger, more alive, that you are impressed with me, hesitant about entering such a family as this, but your desire grows stronger from that thought. You see, I do remember what you're like.

I'll tell you what else I remember. At odd times, on my knees in the kitchen or the bathroom, while sewing a button on a dress, I remember geometry. You're laughing, I know; you remember how excited I used to get about it, how I always understood it faster than any of us. It was some kind of leap I was able to make, no disbelief to suspend—of course a line has no dimensions and it goes on infinitely—of course. Some days I imagine that there are lines all rushing toward me, intersecting at a point in the center of my heart, and the intersection must remain at all times perfect so that if the center moves I move, but the center moves only from one room to the next of my house (winter now, the sky gray and inches away from every window) and, infrequently, to other places in this town where I am expected only at expected times. Of course that is Euclidean geometry, the geometry where lines are straight, the kind that only works on earth. For days I have been trying to remember the name of the geometry that's true for the universe, where lines curve, and that is one thing I can't remember. It frightens me. Last night I took my oldest child into the kitchen. She's in kindergarten and I've already taught her to read. I put a soap bottle on the window ledge, stood her at one end of the kitchen, and asked her what the bottle lined up with on the house next door. She said the living room window at the front of the house and I said correct. I took her to the other end of the kitchen, asked her the same question, and she said the kitchen window at the back of the house. I hugged her, said see, that's geometry, that's how the Greeks knew, without going there, the approximate distance to the stars. She of course didn't understand. My husband understands but is bored by it. When you come we'll talk about geometry, astronomy; we'll discuss physics. There have been new developments, I'm sure, just as I'm sure that you know about them. A few years back I began feeling stupid and I'm hoping you will teach me and once again make me feel bright.

I don't know who to blame for what has happened to me. My husband reaches for me and it's comfortable, but the only way I can respond is to close my eyes and think of you, the sensitivity between us, our hands moving at the same time, the kisses like some sort of gentle dance they were so perfect. The thing that gets me is remembering how innocent we both were, when we thought of ourselves as so modern. Afraid of pregnancy, young, we of course never slept together—it wasn't done then. When you come we will sleep together even if you can't for some reason take me with you. And I will not feel guilty, will not feel guilt, because it will be for the times when we should have but didn't. In the greater scheme of the universe, time is not necessarily a straightforward line or progression—I will think of that moment as happening before my marriage as it should have, and there will be no guilt.

I must tell you. There are women on my street who do not have children and who still work at home. There are

women on my street who do not have children and who
leave every day for work, dressed in expensive clothes.
There are women on my street who do have children
and who still leave every day for work, the clothes only
slightly less expensive. I am not stupid. I know that all of
those options were at one time available to me, that
some of them still are. I am not shallow enough to think
that typing someone's letters is more noble than caring
for children. I know I could do both, have my children
and work. I could teach part-time at the high school.
But last week I found myself throwing out all my physics notes, and I can't remember the name of the geometry that works for the universe, and I can't, cannot move
from this house. As I grew up I spent all my time inside
the house and now my children are growing up in the
house; I can't even push them into the back yard to play.
I'm afraid that when it comes down to it I'm not very
good for them. I'm afraid of that.

Every day I think this is the day I will make a decision
to do something, and every day I am unable to make a
decision. I am waiting for you to knock me out of orbit,
to cause combustion, to make me explode. When I think
about leaving with you, I can't imagine living more than
three or four more years and I am not at all frightened
by that thought. When I imagine staying here, I'm
afraid of every ache, every trip of the foot; I must live
until I'm very old, I must. This makes little sense, but it's
the way I feel. Possibly I don't want you to see me when
I'm old—I know that you would leave me in a while, I
know that and I wouldn't want to live beyond that, having lived my life somehow to avoid loneliness. But the
other, why it's so important to live so long, that I don't

understand. Sometimes I think the stars, the universe, the earth must feel this way, this ambivalence, secure in their circles, their safe fixed cycles, but waiting for the day when the edge of the universe begins its collapse inward (the way paper burns from the outside in) toward the center, first a few stars, then more, a gathering fireball, all the stars waiting and then the rush, the thrill in those eons when they know it's coming, are waiting to be consumed, the exquisite beauty of that chaos and just so, just in that way I expect you at all moments, fear you, and expect you to make me luminous, incandescent for a while.

Banquet

lma sits alone at the table, watching her family
line up for food. She will go last when the line is
shorter. A daughter complains to her husband that every Oktoberfest banquet is the
same, that it takes weeks to rid her clothes of the sour
odor of kraut. The husband laughs, squeezes the
daughter, and whispers something, Alma's sure, about
humoring the old woman. Eat the sweet sausage, he's
saying, buy the children cloth toys stuffed with some old
lady's hose, cast-off shoes covered with macaroni
sprayed gold. Alma says nothing, knows they care for
her really, these older ones who feel the relationship,
knows they're frightened and sometimes angry at what
she might have passed on to them. Lately they give her
pats instead of hugs. She has lived the last twenty-five
years of her life with only one breast. It has been
months since anyone kissed her on the mouth.

A great-grandson sits to her left, gives her an extra roll
he's picked up in line, a sweet sticky roll with the fresh
taste of yeast. Across the table a younger great-grandson's first scribblings dig through the paper cloth in
places to the wood, drawn with his grandmother's pen,
another of her daughters. Soon the table will be filled, a
whole tableful of people there because of her. She never

did, finally, teach school but she did something, didn't she? A granddaughter standing in line wears blue jeans, a flannel shirt. Alma never at church without white gloves, tight between the fingers. But doesn't say anything, remembers her mother saying *Change with the times, grow old with grace.* Earlier that same granddaughter bragged of how she would remain single until she was thirty-five, love a thousand men, and backpack in Europe, then become a mother and a nuclear physicist, said, Grandma, why did you never teach? Looked at her condescendingly, thinking, you could have done all this and you did nothing, poor woman. Alma explained again, the old story, about World War I, about German being taken from the schools as she was coming home on the train, filled with stories of school chums to tell her brothers, a degree from the small-town Indiana college in her lap, wrapped in leather, the degree that would allow her to teach children to speak her mother's language. And then rolling bandages, making socks, John back from the war, marriage, children, but the granddaughter didn't really listen—thought, years have passed between then and now, you could have done something.

This granddaughter wants to move away—to Paris, San Francisco, New York—says there is no continuity, only her freedom, will waste much time fighting her own mistakes, mistakes that Alma could point out. What are generations for if not for that? Alma, amazed, wonders how you face death alone in New York, her own father having told her that the family is like the revolving spokes on a wheel, that you see the spokes rising up behind you and falling in front of you, and when it's your turn to fall you're not afraid because more spokes are rising and the rest of the wheel keeps revolving.

The granddaughter walks over from the line, gives Alma an extra roll, then sits at the other end of the table, afraid to be like her. Can't be helped. And maybe she doesn't remember as much about being young as she thinks she does. Earlier, at the bazaar, she called the eleven-year-old grandson *Schnikelfritz* and kissed him as he stood talking baseball with a friend. He blushed and said, Oh Grandma, and now he comes and sits near her, red at the neck. Like the granddaughter, he spends much time deciding what he will be, though not in as much turmoil, knows everyone will expect him to be something. He talks of space shuttles, atomic power, thinks she knows nothing but memories of tin pails of beer carried to her father in the summer, ice carts pulled by horses. Alma thinks, no, too much emphasis on style, not substance. Widows eating the noon meal after church on Sunday. One had been a doctor, one a secretary, one a housewife. One had been crazy. All talk about the ocean, a pain in the joints, the color yellow, the taste of coffee. It comes down to that. There is that connection between friends. Alma watches her family ladling kraut from the huge kettles to their plates. All of the grandchildren standing unaware of the things that have come from her, a gift. A certain twist of a certain chemical causes the reddish hair, they know that. But there are things that they don't know.

She takes one of the sweet rolls from the pleated and waxed container. The amber liquid sugar settles in a pool at the bottom. Some sticks to her fingers. A grandson has a bead on the tip of his nose, the Reverend stands by the banquet table and smiles, a bit of caramel on his tooth. She smiles back. Clean German Protestant, enormous thighs, she's heard he sweeps the snow off the driveway of the manse every twenty minutes as it falls, and never has to shovel. She had a crush on him once, before the fat covered him like mounds of potatoes. Of course she never told him and never told John, decided not to feel guilty about it as long as it didn't hurt anyone. They were her thoughts and she had a right to them. It made her happy for a whole summer when she was twenty-four and John was thirty and working too hard. She would come into the cool dark church in the afternoons to cut out pictures from picture books for the bulletin board in the cradle room, hoping she might catch a sight of him pacing at the end of a high-ceilinged hall, working on his sermon. She wore a cotton print dress and sat on the cool green linoleum by a crib, very aware of herself. She often laughed at this, knowing that he wasn't aware at all, and glad of it. She would see him in one of the dark halls, first a blur of dark suit and light brown hair, then her eyes would become used to the dark and she could see the serious features of his face in the same way, she thought, that the babies in the cradle room would see the picture of Mary she was cutting out for them, first as a blur of blue that was part of the brown corkboard, then as something separate and finally at the end of two years, as something resembling a real person.

That was many years ago but she still thought of him with gratitude, could sometimes see the young man in the old. He helped her in the years after John died, told her to look for a sign, and she began to sit long hours in the sanctuary washed by the light from outside died deep blood colors as it filtered through the stained glass windows. A ray of royal blue that had once been white warmed her hand as she sat in her pew all that spring after John's death. The sign was this: things change form with ease, with abandon. There was much comfort in that.

Another granddaughter comes to the table, brings Alma a square of dark red Jello, half a pear trapped in the bottom like a small white turtle. Alma thanks her, wants to give her a gift also, points out the steam in the kitchen, a gas that had once been liquid, crowding against the window in the swinging door which leads into the banquet hall, leaving a film of moisture on the glass. But the granddaughter says, That's nice, accustomed to her excesses, doesn't know that Alma's trying to save her years of searching, goes down to the other end of the table and sits by the granddaughter in the man's shirt.

Other grandchildren and great-grandchildren come to the table. Some bring her Jello, others bring her rolls. One laughs, says, We're the Jello brigade. Alma knows she will remember that phrase forever, that that grandson will always be the leader of the Jello brigade. Never one to think of a phrase, she is always the one to make it stick. One of the women at Sunday dinner looked at the table of widows and said, We're the go-go grannies. From that point on, Alma had never issued an invitation to coffee or games of Manipulation or chicken dinners at the Hollyhock Hill without saying, It's the go-go grannies, We're the go-go grannies, The go-go grannies are getting together. Long after the rest of the women had forgotten where the phrase came from, Alma could have told who said it and where, on what Sunday of what month of what year.

Another grandchild comes with a roll for her. He sits and wraps a transparent ribbon of kraut around the tines of his fork, doesn't want to eat it. A son sits across from her and begins telling her how much he's always loved her music cabinet with the hand-painted picture of a man playing a lute on the front. He guesses it must be worth hundreds, a real antique. Sometimes Alma welcomes these comments, wants her things to go to those that want them. At other times she's resentful, thinks they pay much more attention to her things than they used to. She grows suspicious that they're all waiting for her to die, holding their breath. On days like this it seems that they're all talking at once, saying Grandma, I like your monkeypod tray from Hawaii, I like your cloisonné lamp, but you didn't really sell the Tiffany, did you, you do still have the humidor and the cranberry glass? When this happens she can feel her lips getting tight and thin, her eyes getting narrow, and she hears herself ask in a scratchy voice that can't be hers, Why do you want to know? There are things she can't bear for anyone to have. And they're not the important things—her Bible, her pictures of John, the china and cut glass. It's silly things like her rolling pin, the mammy and pappy salt shakers, a metal coffee can where she keeps her saltines, a cotton slip. She knows they won't fare well. She can picture her daughter saying of course *these* things we can throw away. She can see them looking at her earrings—how tasteless, how quaint, how old-fashioned. She can see them laughing at her supply of wine that the doctor told her to drink to build up her blood, a joke almost slapstick, the old lady drinking wine for medicinal purposes. She's told them often enough that she enjoys the wine, has had it for dinner all her life, that the doctor only told her not to *stop*, that it was good for her. The one son who loved to make jokes found her wine the richest material he'd had in years. It was this same son who, when he was twelve and obsessed with being pure and wanted to become a saint, when he stopped eating for a week, had thought her wine was wicked and wild and poured a bottle out in the gravel driveway to save her soul. Alma thinks that she hasn't changed, that if her wine has to be interpreted she would rather be thought of as slightly wicked than as feeble and silly.

And last week in the middle of the night she suddenly couldn't bear the thought of someone throwing away the tiny clear glass bird with the air bubble in one wing and the broken wire sticking out of its breast that John brought her as a peace offering at the end of that same awful summer when she had the crush on the pastor. When he brought it into the dark entry hall, the wire was longer and embedded in a piece of driftwood. They knelt in the hall to put the driftwood on the floor and a thin wedge of light through the letter slot in the door lit only the glass bird, the round glasses on John's face, a lock of his blonde hair, and the diamond on her hand as she touched the bird's left wing. And filled with white light, the wire hidden in the dark and bending, the bird looked as if it flew away from her on its own power, then back to her hand. And she decided that she loved him again, through that bird. Then John placed the bird on her dresser where two days later one of the children, she'd forgotten which one, snapped the wire and left the bird lying in an ashtray. She told everyone she'd thrown it away then, but she kept it in an embroidered handkerchief in her nightstand, ashamed of being so foolish. Then last week she started thinking about it, and she put the bird and the handkerchief in a velvet-lined ring box and went outside in her nightgown to bury the box in the yard. When she came back into the kitchen and poured herself some wine and sat at the table she started to giggle, couldn't stop, wondered how she'd become exactly what they expected of her, a crazy old woman drinking medicinal wine, going outside at night in her gown with a shovel, burying things in her back yard.

The table fills. Everyone eats, the younger ones push the kraut to one side of their plates, wrinkle their noses. One great-granddaughter takes a napkin and dries the kraut juice from the knockwurst she chose instead of sausage, because it tasted the most like hot dogs. One granddaughter, the dancer, taps a tune on her plate with a knife. A son wolfs down his sausage, spears his wife's uneaten sausage with a fork, finishes that, and looks around for more. Alma eats a roll, some Jello, wonders if any of her married children will notice that she doesn't have anything else, decides she'll wait to get more food until someone mentions that she doesn't have any. Before her illness they would have noticed, now they're afraid to look at her too closely. They talk to her of things around her, look at that car, at that photograph, and that's where their eyes rest. A four-year-old great-grandson sitting on her right leans over and says,

Grandma, are you sick? and his mother, putting her arm around him says, No, of course Great-grandma's not sick, she's fine, she'll live forever, and Alma wants to stand up, make a speech, say, Listen it's true and today I'm not all that afraid, things change form, why are you all ignoring it? But she doesn't say anything, because she knows it's hard not to be afraid. She wants to say that it's only something about cells growing too fast. She knows enough to sound scientific about it, she can talk knowledgeably of organs and glands, but she doesn't know enough to stop it from feeling like black magic. And it hasn't been that easy to live with it. A few cells having a grand old time at the expense of her body, not just her body, but her self and everything she saw through her eyes in her own way. One consolation there. Revenge if she wanted it. The earth would lose one way of looking at it. No one would ever listen to her back yard quite the way she did. And that's all the earth has required of her after all—a pair of eyes, ears, a nose, nerve endings in the skin, another organism to sense that it all exists. God required more of her, her husband even more, or sometimes it seemed that way. But the earth required only that she touch, and the earth contained the cell in her that was going wild. For a while she tried thinking of it in another way, that those cells in her throat were life, growth in a knot. The only recourse, she decided, was to feel herself as the cancer, to become the cells, cheer as she felt the explosions in her neck, as each cell lit a new cell, eating a vacuum through her body. The grandson in the khaki coat back from Vietnam, short hair he wouldn't grow so he wouldn't forget, talked about lighting up an enemy, not death. That lighting up was real to her, but she couldn't carry it off. She was wherever the cancer wasn't, it was as simple as that. She couldn't contain it. She couldn't ignore it. She wants to tell her children that, that she didn't will it, that she doesn't want it to happen to them, but that if it does, they can stand it, that things change form with ease, that they should remember the family. She wants to tell them that, but they don't want to talk about it, each one of them positive that he is the one human being in the history of the earth who will never ever die.

The great-grandson on her right leans over to her, blonde hair like John's brushing her arm, and says, Grandma, I'll trade you this hot dog for that Jello, and he pushes a plate of kraut and applesauce and a hot sausage with one bite missing toward her. She gives him two red Jello salads and a sweet roll, saying Take this sweet roll and remember that yeast is an animal that causes flour to rise, and the grandson laughs, Funny Grandma, and takes a bite of the roll, dripping caramel on his clean white shirt.

Rapture

All that Illinois winter she'd been afraid of a coming ice age and now here they were where the last one hadn't touched, where dinosaurs had fled and shrunk in the comfort, the ease of the life, to ruby-throated lizards which skittered across sidewalks, where prehistoric birds dove at the water for fish and plants looked like ancient and protective clusters of swords. She sits here now, in a fresh early-morning restaurant behind a glass wall looking out on the Gulf, on a small peninsula so she can watch the sun rising higher on the water as if she is in Mexico, not Florida. With clear lime water glasses on the tables, oranges in baskets and some on the ground outside rotting, dolphins arcing through the water, and white birds and sails both the transparency and lightness of communion wafers on the tongue, she feels something rising in her, an excitement, a joy in her that is almost difficult to contain. In Illinois the colors had been drab—wheat colors, dirt colors; here they are outrageous reds, greens, yellows. And here the warm air and moisture bathe her, close in around her like a pot so she feels, strangely, aware that she lives. (Her first memory involves water, warm air, and this same feeling. They're by a lake, her mother and father and she. The air that day was greenish-gold, mid-summer, a pleasant lake smell of rotting weeds, still water, and gasoline. Her mother had on a black one-piece suit and the legs cut into her thighs and her arms were round and her skin was blue-white. Her father stood in the water by a motorboat and tried to start the engine, but it kept dying. Later they would get it going and he would give her a ride around the lake, and that was exciting and full of action and she remembers the texture of her father's bare knees and the sticky smell of plastic seats and cool water, but that isn't her first memory, her first memory is the moment right before the engine starts, and it felt, and still feels, like before that she was unconscious and she chose that moment to wake up.)

When the waitress comes, her husband orders coffee, eggs, fresh-squeezed juice, a newspaper. She sees Eggs Benedict on the menu, something she's never had. When it comes and there's a slice of orange and a stalk of asparagus alongside, she feels dizzy from the happiness, as though the orange and the asparagus are signs, another symptom of the goodness here. She tries to explain this to the waitress and to her husband, and they smile at her, her husband turning slowly to his paper, the waitress no doubt thinking she's a tourist, giddy from the climate. She leans back in her chair, rubs her hands over her bare arms, and thinks no, I live here now, this is my home, cold weather will not touch me, nor the cold seasons of the heart. She drinks her coffee, watches a tree full of wild parakeets outside the window, the silver watch on her husband's left arm, his cheek-bones tensing and relaxing as he reads. Last night they had gone outside, around midnight, and gone swimming in the warm water of the Gulf. They had gone far enough away from shore that it felt as though there were only water and sky, both the same shade of blue-black, and holding onto one another, treading water and looking up at the stars, both of them had the same sensation, as though they were swimming through space, like a dream of falling and there's no end to it, but a safe, euphoric falling, like flying. She reaches over now and touches his hand, asks him if it hadn't been wonderful, swimming in the Gulf at night, and he puts the paper down, apologizes for not paying enough attention to her. He says he'll be sorry when his job starts next week, that he might get too tired for a while to do anything like swimming at night, and she says she can't imagine that it could really be like any job he's been used to, not here. He laughs, and they begin to eat. My eggs taste like lemon, she says, sweet lemon. (Days before she had, automatically, tried to remember what she needed to be worrying about, a holdover from the way she used to feel, and she had found that there was nothing, nothing she was worried about. She'd even begun to forget old worries—the dreariness of Illinois, problems as a child—and could remember only the good times, the comfortable times, as though she had taken thread and made a stitch in every pleasant memory she had and drawn them together with the dark places hidden in folds, gone. And she herself is expanding, infinitely, a balloon that is not brittle, that will not break.)

As usual, he finishes eating before she does and sits drinking coffee and pointing out articles in the paper. There are new color photographs in here of Venus, he says. He shows them to her. The joy rises and settles in her chest like something tangible. She feels that she could run, climb mountains, and still it wouldn't be released. How amazing that those colors have been there all along, she says, and no one to see them. Yes, he says, amazing. He says that he might get a telescope, that he might make astronomy a hobby. He had never talked about hobbies in the North, had been so involved in his work there. She touches his hand again, knows she can't begin to explain how wonderful his saying that makes her feel. She turns to watch a dolphin, eats a piece of toast, and listens while he calmly talks about theories of the edge of space, the birth and eventual death of the sun, colliding galaxies, in between sips of coffee. Many scientists now think, he says, that the universe is expanding and will some day fall back into a cosmic egg and then explode again into a new one, will pulsate, which makes time stretch infinitely and allows cataclysmic things to happen, as they do biologically, which we can understand, but only so long in the future that it doesn't concern us and helps us feel less responsible. Some theories, he says, are more reassuring than others. She nods, smiles, thinks that sounds as logical as Superman and the planet Krypton and other science fiction, wonders if she plants a poinsettia now if it will bloom this Christmas, wonders when their grapefruit tree will bear fruit that she can pick in the mornings with a wicker cesta. She can find the Big Dipper and the North Star, and she saw them last night and she's seen them in Illinois, and the Indians saw them, and the Greeks saw them, and that's what she knows about stars. She reaches for her coffee, knocks over her water glass, the water darkening the cloth on the table. She takes the

chipped ice in her hands, puts it in the glass, says just
the same, tell me it isn't true, what you said, about galaxies colliding, the universe erased and redrawn. It isn't
true, he says, laughing. Thank you, she says, I knew it
couldn't be, and she looks out at the water, the palm
trees, a blue heron walking like a cat. She wonders how
he can so calmly think about such terrifying things when
they're so happy here, and safe.

The waitress brings a basket of small pastries shaped
like sand dollars, places it on their table, fills their cups
with coffee. They both lean back in their chairs. Her
husband looks calm, thoughtful. The cookies taste like
anise. She breaks one in half to look for the doves that
real sand dollars have in the center, but the baker hasn't
put them in. She thinks that she would like to open a
bakery herself and make sand dollar cookies with sugar
doves in the center. People would bite into them, unsus-
pecting, and discover the candies, and in that way she
could, possibly, begin to communicate the joy that she
feels now. Her arms feel good to her, the soft cotton of
her dress, the sandals on her feet, her hair, the way the
edge of the tablecloth brushes her knees, the bitter taste
of the coffee, the gritty texture of the cookie in her
hand, the hardness of her husband's legs, his arms, the
soft hollows at the base of his neck, beneath his cheek-
bones; all of these things are good. We'll swim or fish all
afternoon, she thinks, watch the pelicans dive for fish
while we eat dinner on the beach, and swim again at
midnight.

The check comes and her husband pays it. I drank too
much coffee, she says as they leave the restaurant, I feel
like I've been drinking ether. Outside it is hot already,

this early in the day. Everything shimmers. This is heaven, she says. I want to stop in the bait shop next door, he says, so we can fish this afternoon.

The bait shop is a shack, gray weathered wood, filled with plastic lures and the smell of shrimp and glass cases of fileting knives. Thousands of hooks tangle and gleam on the walls. She looks at her reflection in the glass cases, notices that she is smiling and that she doesn't stop. Two men come into the shop. They look alike— short unruly beards, sunbleached hair, leathery skin, sandals, cutoff shorts, T-shirts. They smell like gasoline, the smell of her father's outboard motor that day on the lake, her awakening, all her life, she thinks, comes to this slow awakening. She stares at the hooks on the wall while her husband buys shrimp. She holds onto his arm for balance. Water from his shrimp bucket sloshes onto her hand and she brings her hand to her nose, breathes deeply, to calm herself, the happiness becoming too great somehow, too large. Her husband takes her hand, but he's talking to one of the fishermen about the fishing that day, the good spots, the best type of bait. The other man shows her husband a shark's tooth on a chain around his neck, talks about shark fishing, how a shark had taken the leg of his brother when he was snorkeling in the Keys and how he and his brother try to kill as many of them as they can now, how they take the teeth and give them away as gifts. She looks at the tooth lying on his neck, bleached and white as milk glass. She tries to be frightened of it, to imagine it coming after her, after her husband, but she can't, doesn't believe in it. The man tells her husband that if he'd like to go shark fishing with them sometime to leave a message at the bait shop in the morning and her husband says yes, he'd like that, and asks what time they usually go out, and the man says at night of course, at midnight, that's when all the man-eating fish—the sharks, the smiling barracudas, but the sharks especially—come in near shore. They're hidden by the black water then, he says, but the water is thick with them. Wherever you throw in bait, he says, especially around here, you'll find a shark. Her husband thanks the man, holds onto her as they leave, tighter than he's ever held her, thinking no doubt of their swimming the night before, of the plans they'd had to swim again. She holds his waist as they walk to the car. He is pale but she is ecstatic, thinking only that they had made it through the danger, that last night they'd been swimming in sharks, swimming in them. That what she'd thought was the current brushing her legs could have been the smooth body of a shark, the smooth caress of a tooth, a fin. And her head back, her arm feeling the warmth of her husband, the world pulsing and glowing from the sun, something leaps up in her, finally, like a blind fish that rises and breaks through dark water for one, brief, clean taste of air.

Johnny Appleseed

He told me that his ancestor had left his hard black seeds in neat rows where scrub pine or thistle, cockle or thorns would have grown and that when people stopped just long enough to eat the apples he had planted they felt their feet become like iron and their heads become drugged and when they tried to move, found that they, like the trees, couldn't. And in turn, he said, the people planted squash and corn and ate the apples freely, spreading more black seeds whose roots joined under the earth in dark rivers which spread under the houses which also grew from the seeds, wrapping around children's knees, strangling pipes until they had to dig more and more wells.

And he told me I was still under the spell of those trees of his ancestor and I said I didn't believe that until he said would I leave in the morning with him for Zanzibar and I said no. And he pointed to the trees behind my house, black as obsidian against the darkening sky, and he said the black branches were the rivers from the apple trees, spreading out like sap at this time of night, and that to him they were a cutout in the sky. If I looked closely I could see stars where the bark should be. I looked closely and didn't see stars, but there were stars outlined with gunmetal on the hat he wore and I liked it when he stroked his beard a certain way and I didn't care about the trees or the bark or his illusions. He said he was a direct descendant of Johnny Appleseed, that he had the same name, and that once he had even seen him in a bar in Kansas City, the original Johnny, toting glossy catalogs, posing as an undergarment salesman so he could say "negligee" and "brassiere" to the women who came in. He said that he himself was an itinerant magician, specializing in appearing and disappearing, that I'd already seen one-half of his act. He put his arms on my shoulders and asked was I anxious to see the other half and I said no, I wasn't. Then he asked again if I would leave with him for Zanzibar and I said no, but I'd put him up in the garage for the night. He said that was a trick question; since I'd said no I was in need of help and he would stay around until I said yes. I told him he sounded crazy, I thought he was just a tramp, but he pulled his beard and bent his knee slowly so that rings of cloth crawled up his leg and I thought, what could be the harm? Stay, but only for one night. By that time the cut-out trees had bled into the rest of the sky; there were stars around his head as well as on it.

I pulled a mattress into the garage while he sat crouched on a high shelf watching, hanging by rakes, shovels, hoes. His eyes the same silver gray as the gunmetal, they glinted in the dark unevenly, like crumpled tinfoil. He mumbled while I worked, eyes always on me while he mumbled. I covered the mattress with fresh sheets, sprayed lavender between, set a Chinese enameled lamp on a short table, asked him if he needed a blanket. I tried to ignore his incantations. They started low.

Johnny Johnny Johnny Johnny whoops Johnny whoops Johnny Johnny Johnny Johnny

I placed a piece of chocolate on his pillow.

whoops Johnny whoops Johnny Johnny Johnny Johnny Johnny

Sweet cream in a pitcher beside the bed.

Johnny whoops Johnny whoops Johnny Johnny Johnny

I left him in the garage. I locked the door. The bed had looked nice, like a movie set looks—complete where the light reached, but framed by dark and oil and hard metal beaks of machinery. I tried to imagine him sleeping in it.

I went into the house, opened doors and windows for air, locked screens, stopped by a window and touched the screen with my tongue. It was bitter and the taste lasted. I thought about the song I would probably go upstairs to write about a woman whose only sense was taste. About all the things she could touch with her tongue before she died a tragic death from rare infectious germs.

But when I opened the door to my room, Johnny Appleseed was there waiting, the hat with the gunmetal stars slid halfway under the bed. I asked him how he'd found his way past me. He told me that I hadn't really locked anything, that I'd allowed him to come in. I picked up the hat and put it on the dresser. He flipped open a pocketknife and took out a block of wood from between the sheets. Soon he had wood shavings all over the bed. He said the block of wood had once been a whole tree, that he made tiny smooth rings from the wood, that I would find them useful. I said if you're really Johnny Appleseed, shouldn't you have a bag of seeds? He motioned to the empty side of the bed with the blade of his knife.

I said, if you're really a magician, Johnny Appleseed, show me some tricks. He sat on a moonlit tree limb in the cemetery, carving faces in the bark, chips falling on a stone by my feet. Leaping to the ground, he moved the pocketknife toward my eyes, brandished it in the air. See the lights on the blade, he said. I'm carving chips from the moon. Catch one. I touched a reflection of the moon, buried in the hair on his chest. *Now watch the blade, Johnny Johnny Johnny. See the blade bend, Johnny, stroke it, stroke the blade.* I stroked it. The blade didn't bend. *Stroke it, Johnny Johnny,* he said. He moved my hand along the metal, *stroke the blade, watch it bend.* It's flat, I told him. His face moved closer to mine, the hard edge of his hat brushed my ear, he winked. Isn't it amazing that the blade is bending? he said. Bending to match the contour of the earth, he said. The earth is flat here, I said. It looks flat, he said, but it's really bending; it has to, you know, it has to bend everywhere. Not around here, I said. A circle bends everywhere, he said; it appears flat like the earth, but it's really bending. It's flat, I said. Very very flat.

He tossed the knife at the tree. It folded in half and fell to the ground. He turned his wrist and a wooden ring appeared in his hand, rough-hewn. I'm sure I saw it slide down your sleeve, I said. The satin shirt had rippled, I'd seen it ripple. Sit, he said. I sat on the stone amid the shavings. He slipped the ring over my foot,

around my left ankle. Another turn of the wrist and
another ring appeared, this one smooth sanded, var-
nished. He slid it over my right hand. A larger one
appeared. He slid it up my right leg, around my thigh.
That's enough of that, Johnny Appleseed, I said, I feel
very unbalanced. He slid one up my left thigh and asked
me to stand. I clacked when I tried to walk toward him.
Now where's the trick, Johnny Appleseed? I said. Try to
take them off, he said. I tried and they wouldn't come
off, they were stuck, and I said they must have shrunk
from my sitting on the ground. I said at least-clack
clack-help-clack-me remove-clack clack clack-one from
one thigh-clack. One of the rings slid from my leg as if it
were greased. I'll figure out how to do it, I said. I know
it's an illusion.

He took my hand and led me to a flat gravestone,
pallid white and cold. He chanted *Johnny Johnny* and I
lay down on the stone. The letters were indented deep
in the rock; I could feel someone's name and dates dig-
ging into my back. He lay down, brown curls near my
lips, the wooden ring burning on my thigh. Over his
shoulder was the tree, its leaves silver, fruit as bright
and hard as crystal marbles, cat's eye marbles in my
hands, the clicking limbs. Johnny jump up, be nimble,
be quick. I rolled over onto the grass. His back on the
stone, he said that might be what death feels like. If it
does, then it's not so bad, I said, and I brushed the wet
hair back from his eyes. He said Johnny Appleseed had
planted the apples because he had been afraid to leave
the land to the dead things, the wild things. That his
own destiny was to face them, that he was building a
power, that there was no security for him. He gripped

my hand and stared at the sky; it was filled with clouds
and moving with a violence. I could sense that the
emptiness frightened him. The cemetery was quiet.
Then he threw his legs into the air in an arc, did a kip to
his feet, and pulled me up with him. I fingered the ring
clutching my wrist. Mirrors, I said. You must do it with
trick mirrors.

He came once to watch me where I worked, coming in
late after I'd finished most of my set, wearing the hat
with the gunmetal stars and jeans and a muslin shirt and
a floor-length apron with stenciled colored moons and
seaweed on the bib. He asked for a table up front and
the waitress gave it to him. He ordered a pitcher of
sweet cream and ten ounces of bourbon. His table was in
the light from the stage; he sat in the shadow. All I
could see were his disembodied hands pouring the
cream and bourbon into a glass, lifting the glass into the
air and setting it down. The place I worked was deco-
rated like a speakeasy—dim lights, waitresses in flapper
costumes, pictures of gangsters on the wall. I was
dressed like a moll in a red satin dress, greasy red lipstick. I carried a plastic carbine. I sang old jazz, mostly
Billie Holliday and Bessie Smith, sometimes some of my
own songs that I wrote to sound like that same style jazz.
I was glad he'd come because it seemed to be my chance
to mesmerize him. The satin dress molded my body
with stripes of moving lights, clung tightly to my hips.
There was a slit up the side to my waist and I wore a
black leotard and black hose, though it was difficult getting the hose through the wooden ring on my thigh. My
voice wasn't great, I knew, but was throaty and rich and

my movements were good. Men were always coming up to me after the show, wanting to give me a ride home. I had always said no. I sat on a round table and did a turn, easy with the satin dress. I lay back on the table, legs crossed, carbine on my knee. I caressed the microphone with my finger as I sang, looking over to the table where Johnny was sitting.

> *If I should get a notion*
> *To jump right in the ocean*
> *Aint nobody's business if I do.*

I slid off the table and walked over to Johnny. I stroked his hair with the point of the carbine. It tangled in one place and I pulled it out gently. I still couldn't see his whole face, just half of it with a reddish glow from the floor lights. He was half smiling, elfin. The stars on his hat glowed red, more like planets. I walked away and did a few grinds as I sang, something I don't usually do. I walked over to the upright piano and played with the band during the riffs. I looked at Johnny's table, the glass still rising and falling as if by levitation. Suddenly his fingers began to move fast, at the same rate as mine moved on the piano keys. I looked and gold coins began to slide out from between his fingers and clatter on the table. More and more coins appeared in the air. He dropped handfuls; they formed a mound in front of him. I played more intricate riffs; we began to improvise, the band and I. Playing wilder. More coins appeared. Soon the stage manager focused an amber light on Johnny's table. The crowd thought he was part of the show and they applauded. I noticed the band was beginning to play background to him, slowing when his hands slowed, at times becoming frenetic when his hands began to blur. Birds appeared in the air, flapped around the table, tiny globes of blue lights like moons circled among the birds, cards materialized and vanished and still coins were pouring onto the table and off, clattering to the floor. Waitresses stopped bringing drinks. There were no more conversations. Just the sound of the band and the birds and Johnny's silent seductions. He picked up the pitcher of sweet cream and turned it over on the table. No liquid ran out and when he picked it up again, there was a mound of apples which rolled lopsided and thudded off the table. He squashed one beneath his heel. He reached into the air and held each bird, each coin, each moon with his hand and when he opened his hand they were gone. Then both of the hands moved suddenly, pushing the gold coins off the table. Some of them rolled toward me, landing at my feet. *Oh Johnny Johnny,* I whispered. *Oh Johnny.*

I finished my set and he was waiting by the door when I left. He winked and said, "You know where I can find any bootleg whiskey, baby?" All of that stops at this door, I told him. The illusion stops here, doesn't it? I stepped into the night air. This is real, isn't it? He turned me to face him. The apron was slung over his shoulder. His shirt was unbuttoned, the hair on his chest thick and matted. His hand slid down my satin dress, fingered the ring on my thigh. You make a good moll, he said. I put my hand in his shirt, ran up and down his side. I'm looking for cards, I said. Trick cards. You won't find them, he told me. You definitely won't find them. I felt something cold graze my ear lobe. He produced a fifty-cent piece. Come on, he said, I'll buy you a cup of coffee. I reached for the coin and it disappeared. *Oh Johnny Johnny,* I whispered again. *Oh Johnny Johnny.*

Wooden rings holding back the kitchen curtains, hanging from the ceiling like mobiles. Five wooden rings on each arm which clattered when I moved. One ring hugging my neck, rings hidden beneath tables and chairs, between the sheets on my bed, thin ones between the leaves of books, filling pans and skillets, sandwiched between slices of bread. I sealed a drawer in the kitchen shut, the drawer that contained the knives. I sealed the drawer with paraffin because the knives had begun to bend toward me when I neared them. Without stroking, they were all bending toward me. Knives bending, rings appearing. I stood looking out the window with Johnny Appleseed. I said I see it, Johnny. The trees are bleeding, the sap is flowing. He took out his knife. Stroke the blade, he said. Stroke the blade. It bent upward toward the sky. I see it bending, I said. I see it bending, they're all bending. More rings on my arm, a flat one around my waist. Two more flat ones which circled my breasts. A brass teakettle rocking on the stove like a blind singer. Johnny Appleseed went up to bed. I went to sleep in the garage.

I found a box in the garage, filled with toys, my artifacts. I lay on the mattress, surrounded by stuffed bears with music boxes, brass key wings plunged deep in their backs, rotating like hummingbirds. I caught a wing in my teeth, felt the metal cold and bitter on my tongue, let the notes out slowly. I held a bear to my chest, felt the humming of the song in the bear like a heartbeat. The bears stopped one by one. I continued holding on to them. I saw the door open; I'd known he would come. *Johnny Johnny Johnny Johnny whoops Johnny whoops Johnny.* He sat down cross-legged by the enameled lamp, the light modeling his face. Give me those, he said, it's the only way you'll live. I handed him the bears. He put them back in the box, pushed the box away, outside of where the light reached. He lay his hat over the lamp; it dimmed the light. He slipped off the apron. The shirt beneath was made without buttons and was open at the collar. He pulled it off over his head, the thick hair on his chest, the hair. He turned off the light then; the garage blackened. My blouse unbuttoning, jeans catching on rings. Hands moving up my belly, nipples rising as if by magic. Plant some, Johnny, plant. There is no garage, Johnny, I said. There is no house. No trees. No earth. Just this mattress, cool sheets, your voice in my ear. I can be in Zanzibar, Johnny, I said. I'm already there, I said. And I love it Johnny, it's nothing Johnny, it feels good Johnny Johnny, and empty Johnny, it's real Johnny Johnny, it's real Johnny, it's real.

Rain Forest

For the first time she was aware, though only slightly in the moments when she was still, of a warmth or a rumbling of something happening in a part of her body she'd always thought was her stomach. A part of her stomach, though, that had always been dormant, made no demands of hunger before dinner or pain after, was a hibernating animal stretching, waking, pushing to pull her attention away from a stuffed duck and a red scooter in the same way that once her legs, her arms, her fingers and teeth, when acknowledged, had drawn her from her father's gold pocket watch, the first object of fascination.

Though quiet, the animal grew more assertive throughout the day as she sat in school wishing she could run to free whatever it was trapped inside of her demanding her to look, not at the map of Africa with the rubber-tipped pointer migrating from Senegal to the Gold Coast, following the route of an ancient man long dead, the map, the man, stories of Tarzan and monkeys, elephant tusks and Christ still not fitting into one puzzle, one continent; not at the pointer or the man holding the pointer, but inside, something's happening inside, the animal cajoled, prodded, demanded.

As the teacher moved from the coasts to the jungles,

she felt the steaminess of Africa closing around the part of her body where the animal was waking, the warmth, the moisture of antediluvian creatures rising from muck and living in jungles, eating trees. And dinosaurs. Were there dinosaurs in Africa or were they extinct there, too, and who wanted to know? All that was important right then was the sensation of something happening to her inside, and she was not sure yet whether this awakening beast was something to fear, something to trust, something to ignore, something she imagined, or something just to feel when other things were still, like the thunder always sounding in her chest when she searched for it, the tick of a clock.

The bell rang in the hall, dully, indistinctly, a high mechanical recording of her mother's voice: *Come-home-now-Jeannie, come-home-now.* She left class and headed for the girls' rest room before she walked home and, though it was a ritual she followed every day, today when she stopped to look in the mirror she noticed she looked pale. Was she sick? She splashed some cold water on her face. The wash basins were getting too low for her. She dried her face with a brown paper towel that smelled funny and began to disintegrate in her hand, then threw it away and went into the second stall from the end, wondering if it were true what her older sister said, that there weren't any partitions and doors in the boys' bathrooms.

She absently pulled up her dress and pulled down the plaid shorts she always wore underneath so she could do cartwheels at recess, then pulled down the Carter's underwear with the frayed elastic. She listened to the sound of rain outside and looked at the clean white porcelain between her legs, elephant tusks? She brought her legs together, caught the Carter's where they were sliding down between her knees, caught them before they fell limp around her shoes like a puddle. They felt damp and warm, jungle feeling. She saw a tiny dark hair like a pig's tail on her thigh. She tried to brush it away, but it stayed, it was growing there. It looked funny and it made her laugh. The animal was pushing out through her skin. She pulled the underwear back up. The jungle felt good. She relaxed with it, lay back into the steaminess of it.

She left the stall and looked among the porcelain and chrome for pygmies or amazons, everyone who lived near jungles a result of Alice's wafers. She remembered the words, she'd seen them on the door to the second stall, etched with something sharp, so the metal gleamed through the dull pink paint. She opened the door and looked. There were the words, the quote from the Alice book: the door said, "Eat me." If she did, it would make the mirrors liquid, the sinks taller to her or much smaller; she could swim in her tears. Her pink tongue touched pink paint, dug into the crevice where the paint was missing. The metal sent a shiver through her teeth, but nothing happened. She was still the same size. All of the real Alice wafers must be someplace else, she thought. The steam radiator under the window began to hiss. She left the bathroom, carrying the jungle with her.

She wouldn't tell her mother about the animal, not until she could see it, could touch it, was sure of it as something that existed, not just a feeling that could come and go. She decided that it would surely grow in her like her mother's baby. Her mother had said she had a new baby because she was married, that that's how God knew to give women babies, when He saw they were married. Once a woman on the soap opera had had a baby and she wasn't married; she had asked her mother how that was possible and her mother had told her that the woman must have prayed very hard. Jean had prayed for one for two years and had received a Tiny Tears for Christmas. But now there was this, that had been still, awakening in her. She'd never heard of it happening before, but surely in a world where there were pygmies and elephants and oceans clinging to continents, anything was possible.

The baby lay in a wicker crib outside the door to the sauna in the basement of her house. He lay among blankets, chewing on his fingers, saliva dripping out of his mouth. She took a corner of the blanket and dried his face and he laughed, kicked the blanket off his feet. Since the baby had been born, she had to control an urge to suck her thumb again, something she hadn't done in years, not since her mother had painted her thumb with iodine when she went to bed. She opened the door to the sauna and the dry heat pinched her face. The wooden walls smelled like graham crackers; there were rocks glowing red in the corner. Her mother sat wrapped in a towel, one breast uncovered. She was rubbing oil onto it; it gleamed like polished wood. Her mother covered her breast quickly when she came in. She very seldom saw her mother undressed.

Did you see the baby on your way in? her mother asked. *I love him so much that I could bite him,* she answered. Her mother laughed and asked her about school while she pulled the towel up tighter under her arms and tucked one end of the towel under another so that it stayed up on its own.

Her mother leaned back into the corner of the sauna, an iguana in the corner of a cardboard box at school, the box might tilt, the rocks in the other corner for balance. Her mother peaceful, eyes lizard slits in the heat. There were grainy blue veins on her legs like a map of rivers. Her own legs were milk-white, unblemished, like the painted plaster legs in stores that they used to sell nylons. *Mother,* she said. Her mother said, *Jeannie, would you pour water on the rocks?* She picked up a coffee can with the letters wearing off and poured the water so slowly that the steam rose like a rain forest. Something in her liked the steam. *Mother,* she said, looking down at her own body, *how do you know if you have pretty legs?* wondering as she said it if this would be a new gift, so many things waiting to surprise her, like the day her father had told her she had a pug nose and that that was beautiful, when she'd always assumed that noses were noses. *That's a funny question,* her mother said. *Why don't you take off your clothes and bathe with me?* Her mother leaned forward and ran her hands over the inside of her calves. Jean took off the dress and the plaid shorts and undershirt and climbed up onto the second level. She sat awkwardly in her cotton underpants, careful not to jostle the animal. *Your father says that I have pretty legs, it's hard to say,* her mother said. *Are mine pretty?* Jean grabbed her foot with her hand and extended her leg to the side. *Nine-and-a-half-year-old legs aren't all that formed yet,* her mother said, *they're fine legs. They'll get a shape in a few years, a little swelling in the calf, tiny at the knees and the ankle, why? Just wondering,* she said, *if mine will look like yours or like Daddy's; Daddy's legs are hairy. Women scrape the hair off,* her mother said.

She'd seen her mother in the bathroom, in a terry cloth robe, the hot water fogging the mirror, clouds of white foam covering her leg, running a blade across the skin, saying it may look like a silly thing to do, and probably is, but no sillier than anything else when you thought about it, even breathing for that matter. It was all the same in the end, something to fill your time with. Not important, she said, but she'd seen her mother panic at the appearance of a tiny hair on her thigh as she left for the pool, panic and run back inside for another scrape of the blade, a tiny dot of coagulated blood replacing the hair. *In Africa there are women who cut their faces to make scars in designs,* she told her mother. *See?* her mother said, not referring to anything, and she licked the perspiration from her upper lip. *Pour a little more water on the rocks,* her mother said. *It's getting dry in here again.* Jeannie poured water from the can. The rocks hissed. She climbed back onto the wooden bench. *Why do they call this a sauna bath?* she asked, *you don't take a bath in it. I don't know why,* her mother said, eyes closed, *but I think they do take baths in it in Sweden. They must use sweat for water then, sweat and soap,* Jean said, and laughed. Her mother shuddered and said, *No, they must have buckets of water, they're more civilized than that, horses lather in sweat, not people,* and she unhooked a corner of the towel to mop up the perspiration forming on her chest. *After all we're not animals,* she said.

Her mother changed positions, stretched out on the bench, one leg folded over the other. Jean pulled her knees up and sat Indian style on the bench. *It's really hot in here, isn't it?* she said. She settled against the wall and closed her eyes, conjured a picture of herself a few years older with long honey-blonde hair, no matter that her hair was really almost black; she was wearing a short leather tunic, the fur of an animal not scraped clean enough in places still sticking to the leather, having adventures, being tied to stakes with fire beneath her and being rescued. And then, lying in the middle of the jungle, in a clearing, stretched out in the greenness, surrounded by macaws, jungle birds, and the hot breath of lions, letting herself fall into the moist grass.

She felt the animal stirring again. A slight cramp in the stomach, motion. She said, *Mother, what's it like to have a baby?* and her mother said, *I slept through as much of it as I could. I couldn't stand to hear the cracking bones. I've forgotten the rest; it's a pain you forget. That's all.* The stirring again. She hopes there won't be pain with this, tells her mother that in Africa there are women who don't feel pain when they have babies, that the men do, that the women in the field give birth to a child then pick up a hoe, confusing. Her teacher told her that. The next time she feels pain she'll go to Africa on a safari and give it to someone else. Her mother laughed and told her she'd probably end up with someone else's toothache in exchange, that she can't really believe that story. Jean said she guessed she just wouldn't grow up then, and her mother said she had no choice. She'd already swallowed the wafer. Her mother said if she knew how to stop it she would, and she ran her finger along one of the blue veins on her leg. She said that there were always women turning twenty, women that had been babies when she was twenty herself, that she had babysat for them and let their small hands wrap around her finger and tug, knowing that she was large enough to crush them, and loving them for that. And now, she said, she was sometimes afraid of them, even though she knew it was silly. Jean said that they could all make scars on their faces like those women in Africa and that no one could tell who was young and who was old then and everyone would be pretty. Her mother said that her teachers had been filling her head with stories, that there weren't very many places like that left anymore, that Africa was becoming just like everywhere else, no longer dark and moist, but concrete and steel and men in suits. Jean said she didn't believe that, that when she was old enough she would drop from a plane over the continent and the jungle would catch her like a soft sponge. And anyway, she said, she was really not going to grow too much bigger. And her mother leaned over and hugged her, her nails accidentally making a small scratch on her back, and said, *That's good.*

Jean could hear sounds beginning outside the door, a rustling of jungle grasses. Then the cry of a wild bird. More birds, gathering noise, until the sounds turned into a wail which brought her back to the baby in the crib outside the door.

Her mother said, *Darn,* a harsh word, and slid her legs to the floor while she touched the towel over her right breast. There was a dark wet spot on the towel. Her fingers were wet and she wiped them off on another part of the towel, leaving a wet spot there too. *What's that?* Jean asked. *Nothing,* her mother said. Jean thought she might cry, her mother doing this, not sick? *What is it?* she asked again. Her mother shrugged, smiled, said,

Milk. Starts when your brother cries; I can't stop it. And she opened the door to the sauna and left, saying, *Come out in a minute; you've had about enough heat.* Jean promised herself never to cry again, if it made her mother do that.

She poured more water on the rocks to make more steam and sat back on the bench. She stretched the elastic on her underpants to look at her stomach. A flash of something russet caught her eyes on the white Carter's. It was red, it was blood. The animal must be dying, not waking, and she lay down on the bench and put her feet up on the wall. She wouldn't let it die. In a few minutes her mother came to the door, dressed, and said, *Jeannie-come-out-now,* and Jean whispered, *Blood,* at her mother who looked filmy through the steam. Her mother looked and said not to worry, though it was odd, only nine and a half and after just promising not to grow. And she asked her to sit up so she could talk to her, but Jean wouldn't sit up, she wouldn't let the animal die. So her mother tried to draw pictures for her in the steam condensing on the window, of organs existing where she had always thought only one existed. She reached down and touched the blood and then looked at the slick blood on her finger. This is one story she couldn't believe, it could just as likely be an animal. And she wouldn't let it die and it would never happen again and she thought of the rain and the blood and the milk and the steam and the oceans and blue rivers on her mother's legs and she promised herself that she would never drown.

Cousins

We share some of the same relatives and, if diagrammed, they would hold us together like hinges or bonds drawn in geometric shapes between hydrogen, say, and oxygen in water, or any other elements that fuse. But it's a tenuous fusion; there are many other relatives that we don't share, and if one of these other relatives draws a family tree I am not included, unfastened and set to drift because I am related only in that my mother is sister to their father and my blood does not flow directly to the treasure we all hope to find, hidden in our genes and only waiting to be recognized, some man or woman centuries before whose life was important enough to justify the secret knowledge that we deserve more, much more, recognition from the world than we have ever received.

There is one grandmother between us. They have another, a millionaire's wife with orange pink hair who has been lying in bed for three years from a hip that healed months after it was broken. I had another grandmother who had cancer hidden for ten years behind the denim overalls she wore all summer while she nurtured zucchini, cherries, corn. She died one week after the doctor made her lie down, finally, for some rest. It would be interesting if something could be, but nothing can be, inferred from that. It says nothing about my character or about my cousins'. I am not related by blood to their mother, but we have the same thighs. My oldest cousin is not related by blood to my father, but they share a nose. My own brother does not look at all like me; he looks like a man I saw once, for a brief instant, in a shopping mall, buying a pearl-handled umbrella.

When we were children we could say that we were good friends, close friends. At Christmas, the oldest girl cousin and I got matching dolls from our shared grandmother. There is a photograph at the bottom of a glass paperweight in my mother's bedroom where the three cousins and my brother and I are falling out of an over-stuffed chair. We look like we know each other well. At age eleven I got very fat and had a permanent that was too tight; then I got tall and thin. Five years later, when she was eleven, my oldest cousin did the same thing. For a while she was like a spring following me. When we were children I knew them so well that I could have summed up each one of them in a sentence if I had been asked to, looking past those things that were contradictory until I found what was continuous. I could say that the oldest one cried tears without making a sound, the middle one cried with more sound than tears, and no one had ever seen the youngest one cry. If you knew these things about them, then you knew everything you needed to know.

But there seems to come a time when the relationship between individuals becomes set, a concrete wall, when past that point if one of the individuals changes it demands change in all of the others, a recognition of the change, a breathing. And if the others refuse, the wall breaks down into separate blocks and that is all. In the case of my cousins and me, the breakdown is my fault, although it's possible that I am making myself too central, that actually, because I am five years older than the oldest of them, I am only on the periphery, an observer, unimportant. I admit that possibly each one of them and my brother and I would all rush to assign the guilt to ourselves, that it does underline our importance, but in this case I can't help feeling that it is truly I who have caused it because they are the ones who have stayed in the same place, the same houses, and done nothing more than grow older and I am the one who moved away and have tried to come back, but never for good.

The summer before I left for college was when our relationship was set for me. I was the only teenager; my brother and our oldest cousin were twelve. At dinner they performed for me and for each other. When it was my turn to perform, I gave them secrets: names of rock groups, clothing stores, high school teachers that would serve as passwords, keys to the exciting life they supposed I led. I grew used to being the sage, used to the openness of them, the transparency of children. Then I left for college, came back for brief visits, graduated, began to work in another state, and—returning for visits at Christmas and Thanksgiving—found that I was becoming obsolete, that the secrets no longer resided in me. I was no longer needed. I am ashamed to admit that I was hurt by this, found it difficult to speak with them. It was difficult for me to change. I suppose that I am selfish or too easily intimidated. Perhaps I am shy. They were different people, aware of themselves, able to think about their actions secretly at the same time that they performed them—a definition, I suppose, of adulthood. It seems so much more alienating when you watch it grow, when there is suddenly something that needs to be broken down between people who were, at one time, close. I suppose that parents feel this, I'm not sure. I know that it is profoundly sad. With strangers it is more easily broken down. There is no false assumption that you know each other, that it is not necessary to begin at the beginning.

And worse, there is the feeling, unthinkable, that we are the seeds scattered by a single tree, in the hopes that one will take. William and Henry James are a rarity. There is only one Joyce, one Shakespeare, one Pasteur, one Michelangelo. Raised as we were, similarly, we cannot occupy the same space. As teenagers, all of our ambitions ran deep. Only mine are becoming tempered by the demands of practical things. I am slowly beginning to realize that teaching is not something that I make my living at temporarily until I become a famous actress, a playwright. It is what I do, what I am. My cousins do not want to hear this, that it might happen to them. I had been sent out to test the waters, and am no longer trustworthy. Perhaps I am exaggerating. Perhaps I am feeling, right now, the price of my restlessness.

Early this year their father died, my uncle, my aunt's husband, my mother's brother, my grandmother's son. It is important that he is understood in this way, how he was connected to all of us, because he had been the central bond. He had had a heart condition for years. Still, his death was unexpected. He was in his middle

forties, slender, handsome like one of the singers my mother loved, Perry Como—a slimmer Frank Sinatra. He had given up salt and Cokes and this was supposed to have protected him. My aunt found him slumped over a stove that he was moving into his appliance store.

At one time he had wanted to be a pharmacist. Every man I knew who was his age, my father's age, had wanted to be a doctor or a pharmacist. But they had all gone into business. My own father, who started his studies in pre-medicine, spends his life writing reports on the viscosity of nail polish, the solidity of brushes. The only ones who remembered these ambitions, who spoke of them often as if they were still alive, as if they formed part of the characters of the sons, were the grandmothers.

I thought of pharmacy when my mother called to tell me of my uncle's death and I thought of my cousins as they had been when we were small children. This one's an actress, my mother would say, this one a doctor. This one's a poet, this one a composer, this one a politician, my Aunt Mary would counter. I asked how everyone was taking it and my mother told me that my aunt and my grandmother had both collapsed, but that they were doing better now. There are so many "I's" in this that it will be difficult to believe that the real action is going on elsewhere, where I am not. I can imagine the slumping, the collapsing, the initial grief, but I cannot convey it clearly. I am afraid of flying, of the loss of control, it is possibly the thing that keeps me in one place for any period of time, but I flew home that afternoon. By the time I arrived, people had begun to pull themselves together, to behave as though they were calm. No one knew how to act as, here too, the real drama took place in the places where we are separate.

The funeral seems important in the history of my cousins and me. The funeral home was huge—subdued lighting, gleaming parquet floors. I had never seen such furniture, such carpeting and drapes. There were boxes with tissues sticking out like sails or pale limp hands, lying discreetly on marble-topped tables; hidden in odd corners, small private rooms for crying.

I can see my grandmother sitting on a pink velvet antique chair. She has chosen the lowest chair in the room and still her feet don't touch the floor. There are no longer any stores in town that carry her shoe size, and she is wearing a larger size with cloth stuffed into the toes and her white legs are swinging, ever so slightly. The last time I saw my uncle, a year and a half ago, she was buttoning the top button of his winter coat, turning up his collar. She and my mother are both wearing navy blue. It is proper, my mother says, but not as dreary as black. She is a few inches taller than my grandmother. Some day her shoe size also will be extinct. They are both sitting there holding white gloves, with their hands folded over their purses. Before we left the house they had come into my room again and again, asking whether this necklace was too gaudy or these earrings were becoming. For lunch we had cantaloupe and cottage cheese, carefully garnished with parsley. My grandmother leans over to my mother and asks if she thinks the cantaloupe will set well on their stomachs. My mother says she's sure it will and my grandmother sits back up, comforted. My aunt and my oldest cousin wear slacks, simple blouses, and when they first arrive the rest of us look overdressed, showy. Mary doesn't own a dress, my grandmother whispers to me, a little too loudly.

We walk into the room where my uncle is lying in a mahogany casket. It is obvious from the way one cousin touches another's arm or the arm of my aunt that they have bonded together, that when they turn they put on their calm looks, the looks reserved for strangers. I feel like an outsider. We begin to look at each other, briefly, then at the flowers, and we move to the back of the room, away from the body. We circle the walls, looking at the cards as if we are at a museum. How lovely, I say to my oldest cousin, these roses. And these, she says, these apricot glads. I look at her shoes, half a size larger than my mother's, the same size as my own, and I wonder if the world will outgrow us also, as if everything contains some magical yeast, some incredible fermentation, and the women in my family are being left behind, and I almost say something like this to my cousin while looking at a brass goblet, some roses, some cut glass. The boy cousin leaves us, moves to sit in a chair near his father. He straightens his tie, is careful with the jacket of his suit. He will have nothing to do with our talk of flowers.

I see the room filling with people. Each of the family members is surrounded by satellites, friends, distant relatives. When friends come, we are animated. It is wearing, this talk, but we find ourselves interested; we are amazed at how some people are so young still, how some are so old. For long periods of time I forget that my uncle is there, my eyes never moving to the front of the room. I hear Aunt Mary laughing and watch her Indian wrestle with her daughter's boyfriend. My words begin to come easily; I walk up, excited, to where the boy cousin is sitting, watching his father, but when I get there all I ask is the name of a flower, the waxy looking red bloom that is shaped like an ear. He shrugs, will keep his vigil, and I wonder why I did not say more.

Our grandmother, suddenly afraid that there might be something to religion and wanting him to be comfortable, her son, asks my aunt if we shouldn't have a proper funeral. My aunt says no, a small gathering at the gravesite, maybe a psalm, and after that no dinner, no gathering. I overhear the middle cousin whispering to a friend. What is this called, what we're doing? Is this a wake we are having? We have no names for tradition.

I see my middle cousin, her hair the color, the cut of Jean Harlow's. I show her where there are Cokes downstairs. We sit on a sofa and I ask her where she's going to go to college when she is through with high school, what she'll do after that. She shakes her hair, stretches her long legs in front of her, says that she plans to go into music, that she hopes to write a Broadway musical, an opera, a symphony. She says that she will keep her father's name, that she will never change it for any other man. She tells me that she changed the spelling of her first name two years ago, from a "y" on the end to an "e." She says she noticed that I spelled it the wrong way on all the Christmas cards I sent the family, but that I can keep spelling it that way because she is changing it back to "y." I feel absurdly angry at this. I want to tell her, of course, that I should have known, that it was the same thing her older sister had done at her age, the same thing I had done, that it was not, as she felt, original. I want to tell her that she may not have the strength for that, that her talent may not be as great as she suspects. And because I hesitate before I wish her success and because I find, when I do say it, that I do not at that moment mean it, I suddenly am convinced—even though for me the idea of sin has little substance—that what I am feeling is somehow, inexorably, sinful. My cousin leaves and I wonder if everyone becomes this confused at funerals, and I remember a cousin of my mother's who, at the death of their grandmother, seemingly bothered less by the presence of death than by the realization that she was, herself, fully alive, left her husband and children and became legendarily promiscuous for a time.

Later, six or seven of my grandmother's friends come in a group. They have been at a birthday party of the oldest one of their friends. They are all my grandmother's height. They had walked together on the first day of grade school. They tell me these stories. The phone wires flame between them, every day, in different patterns. Each day they make a connection. Here I am surrounded by people who know each other well. Most of the people I have known keep friends for three or four years and then someone moves, or everyone moves. At first we write letters and then we stop. And if we run into each other a few years later, we are different people. I can't imagine what it would be like to have a friend for over sixty years, if I would begin to know what is the same about me from decade to decade, if I would have the depth that is necessary when you're not always starting over. Two of my grandmother's cousins are in the group. They have grown up together, gone the same ways, belong to the same clubs and women's groups. One would not join without the others.

The time for visitation ends and two men in black suits clear the room of people and we are forced once again to stand by the casket. My aunt stands by her husband, looking like a girl, face flushed from the talk, excited. The muscles melt as one of the men from the funeral home puts a crank into the casket, waiting for us to take a last look at his handiwork before he lowers the lid, as nonchalant as if he's offering us, please, one last chocolate. I remember that my uncle's blood has been drained from him, that he has been denied even the comfort of his own blood, and I think of that same blood in all of us, bits of tubing cut and fastened, then unfastened.

He looks so pretty, my grandmother says, still holding onto my mother, he looks so peaceful. He's dead, my aunt says, just dead and that's all. Her shoulders slump forward. The man in the black suit begins to lower the lid slowly and we all huddle together, touch arms, bits of glass coming together finally in a pattern. On my arm I can feel the texture of skin through the soft blouses of my oldest and middle cousin and it feels like my skin. I feel my face and it is a cousin's face; my mother's voice is in my throat. And I think that there is no one I love more than this. *Please God, let them be as great as they can be. Keep the old ones strong and the young ones strong, and when one goes, as this one, please God, let him live within us so that we are greater, not smaller, from his passing.* Then cousins break forward, a last look. And then we all break apart, head for separate cars.

In the morning we watch two young boys in paint-splattered jeans and khaki jackets try to crank the casket into the vault. They have difficulty getting all four sides level and I think that if we weren't there they might let it fall and be done with it. They get it down finally, with much banging and chipping of mahogany, and there is silence, a green wind, and I think that I can hear my cousins' voices but am afraid that I am only hearing my own. And then my cousins and my aunt get into their car. My brother gets into his, Aunt Mary's father into another. My mother and grandmother take me to the airport and they return to their homes.

At Christmas we all get together, but it's built up again and we've lost the stimulus to break it down. We rush through dinner, gifts are sparse, several of us have the beginnings of a cold. We are dressed carelessly. Later we will all wash our hair to go out with friends. When it's time to leave we feel relief. It is a scene we will repeat many times.

The Invention of Flight

I live in a town slowly turning into dust. Choked, finally, by the fields which surround it and by a larger town a few miles west which kept growing like a fat old man adding chocolate to chocolate who, one night in bed, rolled over and gently, quietly crushed his wife. The dust is from the houses rotting, the streets unpaved and rotting, pollen thick as fog, grain elevators pouring out the slick sweet dust of rotting corn until that time in the fall when the fields become white and brittle as bleached bones and the corn is cut close to the roots.

There are only a few stores left in town: one small grocery which doesn't sell perishables, one store full of seed spilling out of bags, one store of dubious nature selling only bait and red cream soda and run by a man known as Cowboy with dust like black seeds in the creases in his neck, age cutting into his face, who dreams he is popular with the farmer's daughters. They in turn dream of winning 4H ribbons at the state fair, of dances at the Legion where boys, farmers' sons, dress in tight pants with silk shirts and sing rock and roll, hoping to be discovered and eventually see mythical places like California. Instead, always, marrying one of the girls when they're sixteen, seventeen, moving into a house that someone has left vacant, buying one car that runs and one without wheels that they put in front of the house on cement blocks, for years keeping the dream alive that they will work on it, make it hot, take it to a drag race in Kentucky. For some reason there are refrigerators on all of their porches.

The county boasts two or three of the rarest denominations of churches, churches where the women never cut their hair and have it done up once a month in the most elaborate tall beehives, the back woven like a checkerboard, churches where the people believe that the walk on the moon was a hoax, something done with mirrors and special animation, that soap operas are more real than the news. A photographer from the capital drove through the town last year and took pictures, looking for quaint and not finding it but taking the pictures anyway, called it a village at peace with itself and in the article placed us in the wrong county and none of us corrected him. It also didn't mention in the article that we are perhaps the closest town to where Wilbur Wright was born, that the air is filled with planes and we have no tourists. Often I feel that I am the only one in the town who remembers that Wilbur Wright began with a bicycle and he rose.

I own a home behind the Holiness church, have lived here for years but am planning on leaving. I'm waiting for the right time. I rent two rooms in the back of my house to two women—a mother and a daughter—and their rooms are stuck like barnacles on a house which is for the most part airy, white, uncluttered. The mother fills her room with Wilbur Wright memorabilia—photographs, clippings from magazines, chrome airplane mobiles, airplane ashtrays, airplane soapdishes, airplane models—in hopes of opening a small museum when the tourists find us, which she is sure will happen in her lifetime. On the wall is a reproduction of a clipping from a local newspaper at the time of Lincoln's death: *Lincoln! The Savior of a Race and Friend of All Mankind! Triumphs over death, and mounts victoriously upward with his old familiar tread!* When I die, she often says, I want the news greeted with this kind of optimism.

The daughter, Melissa, has painted her room a dark moss green and keeps the blinds drawn so that it is barely possible to see the lace bedspread and flowered dust ruffles. A thirty-five-year-old virgin quite tied to her mother, her hair cut with less care than I take to cut the nails on my dog, shapeless faded dresses, she has rounded shoulders and her eyes are always to the ground or red with what, despite her silences, has to be caused by private dramatic bursts of weeping. Her room too is full of objects and, in fact, the only time that I have ever seen any of the feelings which are kept so completely below the surface is when she came out of her dark room one day and, watching to make sure no one saw her, placed a cupid from the vast collection of winged creatures which filled her room on a nightstand in her mother's room and left, thinking her mother would never notice, as if it had flown there on its own. But her mother found it, ran her hands through her hair and across her large thighs, and huffed and said, *Oh these cupids, I hate these cupids, these damn fat little angels,* and picking it up, placed it inside Melissa's door—not on a shelf but in the dust under the bed.

The mother sells Tupperware, Amway, Mary Kay Cosmetics, her afternoons spent in front of a television and most mornings and evenings spent with gray hair perfectly curled and sprayed, going from door to door and from one gathering of women to another, selling things on the home party plan, leading the obligatory word games to give the illusion of camaraderie before bringing out the collection of plastic boxes or creams. The mother is happy, content. She belongs to many clubs and is the one who always insists, at the formation of a new one, that bylaws should be the first order of business. She is, I believe, absolutely without any inner life and without any sensitivity to Melissa, cheerfully bringing up subjects which pain her—the state of Melissa's appearance, the way the world is filled with evil. The mother is so happy and the daughter in such obvious misery that I am convinced the mother has in some way made Melissa the way that she is, that it is she who is completely responsible for what Melissa has become, as if she gave birth to her to absorb her spirit; I am certain there is no love between them.

I sit at the breakfast table with Melissa, trying to engage her in conversation. She smiles, nods, spills tea on her bathrobe as she listens to me talk about the weather, movies, gardening, comfortable subjects.

"This town was once world famous for a type of rose," I say. "They were used to cover the ceiling of the Hilton in New York when Prince Something-or-Other of England came to visit. The roses had buds as big as fists and stems as tall as a child. An adult woman could attach a rose to her waist and the stem would drag the ground."

I am repeating a story I heard from an old woman who was probably lying, but it's a good story and it seems to cheer her.

The mother comes into the kitchen holding an old ventriloquist's dummy away from her body, says, "Look at this filthy, disgusting thing," and puts it in the middle of the table. The dummy is unclothed and sexless, pinched in where the arms and legs meet the body and again at the knees and elbows. The body itself is cloth and stained badly, the head fitted with goggles, an aviator cap. "Found it at a yard sale," she says. "It's going to be Wilbur Wright."

She pours herself some cereal and begins eating. Melissa looks away from the dummy, which is directly in front of her. The mother brings up the years she lived in Florida near Sarasota where circus freaks go to retire. She fills the kitchen with vivid descriptions of the odd people, the deformities that she saw, a 500-pound woman who lived next door to her whose yard was filled with broken clown equipment, tiny bicycles and masks and miniature cars, the mother never able to figure out why. When she begins to describe a dwarf she saw once in a drugstore, how he kept his freezer filled with squirrels, a delicacy, Melissa excuses herself, turns pale. She starts to leave the kitchen, turns at the door and asks me what happened to the roses. I say I heard they were some kind of hybrid and they reverted. They were the only roses known to have reached that size and no one could grow them now. Melissa holds onto the doorknob, turns herself around and leaves. The mother says, "When I was carrying that girl she turned every which direction, you wouldn't believe. I'd say, 'Get down, you son of a bitch,' push her away from my ribs, give her little smacks. I thought she'd have more spunk. When she was born the doctor had to whack the hell out of her to get her to take in air."

I ask the mother to please take the dummy off the table and she does, putting it on the floor beside her chair. I clear my cup off the table, watch as the mother finishes eating and gets up, re-forms a curl of hair near her ear and picks up a pink sample case from behind the door. "The dummy," I say, and the mother comes back to her chair, picks the doll up, slings it under her arm. By this time Melissa is back in the kitchen waiting for her ride to work, her hand shaking as she fumbles with her collar. The two of them leave and I finish getting ready, straightening, finally getting into my own car and driving through town. I watch the old women sitting on front porches. Fuschia plants with globular pink flowers, the florist's tags still on them, hang obscenely above their heads; sharply angled front porch steps have crumbled overnight into dust. If I'm not careful I will think about Melissa during the day, remember the way she looked when she came back into the kitchen, the chalklike powder to cover the redness around her eyes, the way she was bent over and dressed in an old woman's flowered dress and old cardigan sweater, a graying handkerchief showing in the pocket. I know I will not be able to understand why Melissa affects me so deeply, why I can't simply let her live her miserable life in the back of my house and go on feeling comfortable about my own life, the possibilities for the life I am creating for myself. I remind myself that I can move freely in the world, that I have the beginning of a good career and a small circle of friends, and that the only failure, the only possible failure or limitation is the failure of imagination. But there is something in me that needs to release Melissa, to shake her, make her spin. And I'm not sure why I myself am here, how I ended up here, why I stay. I grew up in a city and my inner resources depend on external things; I'll be the first to admit that. I begin to feel a heaviness, fear the morning will come when I'll wake up certain there is nothing beyond this town and so nothing in it, and the dust will begin to replace the air as I breathe, less deeply every day.

Melissa changes into her bathrobe as soon as she gets home from work, lies down on her bed with the blinds drawn. I fix myself a glass of wine and a tomato sandwich, sit and read the paper. The mother arranges samples of soap in a black cardboard box. Every few minutes I hear the springs squeak on Melissa's bed and the water run in the sink in Melissa's bathroom and then again the sound of the springs. After an hour, I put down the paper and knock on Melissa's door. I hear the sound of the faucet again and quick movement and Melissa is at the door, bathrobe buttoned unevenly, squinting in the light, the impression of the bedspread on the left side of her face. I ask if I can come in and she laughs nervously, backs into a shadow, says, "Of course, please."

The room smells of old lady lavender and plastic roses. I go to the window and open the blind, raise the window to let in some air and immediately I feel better, look around to see if Melissa feels it too, this release, but she is huddled against the headboard of the bed, a pillow clasped to her stomach. "How would you like to go to a movie tonight?" I say. Melissa bows her head, smiles, says she has other plans but thank you very much. I pick up a white china cupid from the dressing table and press my finger on the point of the wing, decide to face things directly and say, "Melissa, won't you tell me what's wrong?"

Melissa looks concerned, reaches out toward me as though I'm the one who needs comforting, says in a soft voice, "I hope I'm no trouble to you." She gets up from the bed and goes to the closet, takes out an old wool skirt and lace blouse, picks up her thick glasses from the nightstand and puts them on, smiles showing the pink gums and hastily put-in teeth, the brown hair absolutely without highlights around her shoulders, the child's body. "I must get dressed now," she says. "I hope you'll excuse me." And she pulls the bathrobe tighter around her waist. She smiles like a nun, holds her hand to her throat as I leave and shut the door.

The mother's room is wide open and filled with light. She stands looking into a mirror, applying red lipstick, a flowered pantsuit tight across her rump. She turns to the side and pulls in her stomach, hits her hip with the flat of her hand, says, "Too fat, all Pentecostal preachers' kids are fat, can't be helped," and she backs into a chrome mobile of biplanes.

"Why does she turn on the faucet all the time?" I ask, and the mother shakes her head, says, "Beats me, she's a strange kid." I pinch myself, think: you could do more to help her, you old witch. The muscles tense around the dimples in the mother's fat arms and she turns to me, says, "She's fine, honey, she's living her own life," and I say, "That's no kind of life," and I leave the room.

Later the mother leaves with her sample case. The door to Melissa's room stays shut. I go out into the back yard to water down the dust in my garden, see a vague outline of Melissa sitting by her bedroom window in a straight chair, dressed for the evening.

I drive to work the next day and notice the trailers and small boxy houses folded in among the fields. It seems impossible for anyone to live in those things. I wonder what those people do with their time, what they enjoy. I hate it, the meanness of it. The artificially too-pink cupcakes in grocery stores, women with pasty faces going through the cheap clothes in a K-Mart, the heart-breaking way a woman will suddenly squeal over some hideous plastic flower arrangement, plastic grapes, a conch shell spray-painted phosphorescent green and wired up as a night-light, saying isn't this beautiful or isn't this cute until I want to scream or to cry. I close my eyes and imagine a cloud in a champagne glass, a rose in a bell. I am doing well in my job; in another year or two I will be able to sell my house and find a better job in a city where I can wear fine silk blouses in the daytime, dance at night, never get the deep lines in my face, live the mean existence.

I unlock the door to my office, wait for the first client. The walls are covered with what I know are fatuous posters covered with butterflies and contradictory slo-gans like "Grow Where You Are Planted" and "To Fly You Have to Leave the Cocoon." Whenever I run into one of my clients months after he's stopped coming in to see me, the client will always say, "I'm doing well—it was that poster, the one directly behind your head," or "the one in the corner," or "the one behind the Swedish ivy." Or sometimes one will say, after I've worked with him for months, helped him get food stamps, a job—"It was the Rex Humbard Gospel Hour; it changed my life."

An old man comes in and takes out his hearing aid, puts it in a box. He begins telling me about his girlfriend who is twenty years younger than he is, how he thinks she's seeing another man. He writes country western songs, takes a sheet of yellow paper out of his coat pocket and begins to sing. I point to my watch; his hour is up. He leaves. One after another, they come into my office. A young girl who thinks she is unhappy because she fell in love with the newspaper's picture of a locally infamous wife-murderer. No matter that the only picture they had to print was his high school graduation picture, and the man is now fifty years old; she is sure her life has ended. I listen to them. I direct them to different agencies. Often, through the day, I am struck with how little I have in common with this person or that. Often, through the day, I think of Melissa.

It's dusk and on the sidewalk in front of my house the mother is moving on roller skates. She almost falls and catches onto a tree. She is ecstatic. "I saw a picture in People magazine," she says. "It's all the rage." I hate that phrase, and I hate it that there's an enormous woman on roller skates in front of my house. I particularly hate the fact that this enormous woman looks so happy, but I smile at her, try to find some sympathy for her, and fail. Inside, the door to Melissa's room is, as usual, closed. I pick up a dustcloth and begin dusting—not only the tops of furniture but chair rungs, table legs. The cloth soon becomes so saturated that the dust simply flies into the air, settles somewhere else. I think about typing up resumes, applying for jobs someplace where life is really being lived, decide that I don't have the proper kind of paper, that I'm tired and will go to sleep early. I put the cloth away, put on a nightgown, get into bed, and feel the cool cotton of the sheets on my legs, the faint smell of bleach. I fall asleep thinking about a man I once knew; I fall asleep to the scratching of the mother's skates on the sidewalk, the thump of the faucet being turned repeatedly on and repeatedly off.

An hour or so later I awake to the sound of singing coming from the Holiness church. I get up and look out the window, see the church windows lit yellow, men with blue suits and pale necks, women in dark dresses and serviceable shoes. Every now and then one of them gets up and walks to the front of the church. Some of them are crying. I sit on the floor next to my window, the warm air on my arms, my face near the rust smell of the screen. Two teenagers are sitting on the curb in front of the Coke machine at the gas station. The boy reaches over and touches the girl's hair, slides his finger along the nape of her neck. I notice Melissa sitting in the back yard, a glass cupid in her hand, looking at the church, looking, as I am, at the teenagers. The mother comes around the side of the house, puts an arm around Melissa; Melissa shakes her head, and both of them come inside. I think about one of my clients, a young woman who had gotten married at about the same age as the girl sitting on the curb. Two years later she had two children and no husband.

She began to go to the bars in the adjoining town, began to abuse the children. I had to put the children in foster homes. The woman changed then, found a job, put up with her friends' teasing when she wouldn't go into town, finally got her kids back, lives what seems to me such a boring life, such an incredibly simple life, is still fighting herself and not really happy, but braver than I'll ever be. It's difficult for me to understand. My friends tell me to leave, to fly, to find someplace else to live, that my life will change. And I think of that girl, how she fights to stay in a worse situation than I am in. I wonder how someone else would look at me, at my life. I try to believe that life is rich and understandable and full of possibilities, that what people do is chosen, that they can choose again, and it's difficult to think that in light of Melissa, in light of the fact that she is real. It's tempting to think there are people who can live like she does, that I'm special. The mother thinks that way. When a young couple down the street were arrested for drugs, the police knocking over pots of geraniums in their excitement and clumsiness, the mother talked about it for days, and I tell her I feel sorry for them, for the shame of it. She says, "Oh, I don't think it bothers their kind, do you?"

The girl on the curb cups her hand under the boy's chin, her hair reflecting the yellow light from the church; her laugh cuts through the singing. An airplane flies overhead; I can blot it out with my finger.

The locusts begin their noise; the pollen is choking. I had made a vow to leave by fall, but it's late August and I've done nothing. Half the people in town get their trees topped for winter fuel, and the town is full of

amputees, the sidewalks littered with carnage of twigs
and sawdust. Both children and insects seem to multiply
geometrically. Insects run into screens, walls, people's
heads, crazy with dying. Children topple their bicycles,
run into the streets, into old women with packages until
they are finally gathered into the vaults of yellow buses
taking them to another town. I like to think that one of
them will spend her time daydreaming, designing pre-
tend-rockets, golf courses, fuel-less lawnmowers, rock-
ing-chair generators. Think of it: centuries and centuries when no one thought of how to fly and now the sky
is filled with men and women flying.

In a field by the grain elevators, the Nazarene church
sets up a revival tent, brings in a fattish preacher with a
charismatic voice in the rhythm of preachers. His voice
over the cold blue metal of microphones joins with the
locusts. Every night there is healing. Women with the
odd small-town combination of shoulder-length stringy
teenage hair, stomachs large from childbirth and cake,
lined grayish faces, smile like young girls in love. I can
see the tent from my window, hear the shouting, the
release of something in the people inside. For several
nights the mother goes to the tent, comes back late with
a look of high adventure.

I spend a lot of time on my porch swing watching,
listening, am not moved, only curious. The locusts, the
sound of the revival, the children in the streets, a neighbor sanding a car, the strangling sound of Melissa's faucet and then, a strange thing, the squealing of trucks,
twenty or so, pulling into a cornfield across from the
revival, knocking over corn pale green and scrawny
from heavy spring rains. It's dark and I can't tell what's

going on except that the trucks circle and people get out of them, begin hammering and moving.

The mother comes out onto the porch with the dummy, completely outfitted now, on her hip, a box of airplanes in her arms. "What's going on?" I ask her, knowing that she would know.

"Poor Jack's Amusements," she says. "They're setting up here this year. We're going to have a fair."

I laugh. "This place looks like the bombing of Dresden; half the buildings in town only have one wall. Where are the people supposed to come from?"

"They'll come," she says, "and I'll be there waiting."

The mother heads toward the trucks. Melissa comes out onto the porch, sighs, sits down on a step to watch. Her face has no expression; the eyelids now and then slip slowly down over her eyes and I think she's asleep for a second or two until they open again, just as slowly. On some days something will excite her for some reason, will almost make her happy, and her upper lip will shake. Often she holds her throat, and it breaks my heart.

"How long is the revival going to stay there?" I ask her, thinking that she probably won't know. "For another week," she says.

For some reason this strikes me as funny, the whole thing, and I laugh again, make the swing bounce, hug my knees. Melissa is wearing a brown sweater buttoned up to the chin, but she pulls it tighter. "Don't you think it's hilarious?" I say to her. "Things are going to get crazy around here." She smiles and touches her neck, touches the peeling porch paint, smoothes the hair back from her forehead. She gets up and touches my shoulder, sighs, and goes inside.

The mother comes running up the sidewalk then, a curl of hair broken loose and bouncing dangerously close to her mouth. She's sweating from the exertion, still holding the dummy and the airplanes. "They're going to let me set up a booth," she yells. She begins to talk rapidly, backtracking in her story, going off on tangents, the dummy hanging precariously by his feet on her arm. They're going to let her set up her airplane collection; apparently she's convinced them she is a ventriloquist who can tell fortunes, a ventriloquist with some kind of Wilbur Wright gimmick.

"Watch me," she says, sitting down on the porch step, in the place where Melissa had just a second ago been sitting. She puts the dummy on her knee, straightens the aviator cap. *Hello,* the dummy says in a high-pitched woman's voice. *My name's Wilbur. What's yours?*

"Did my mouth move?" the mother asks.

"Did the dummy say that or did you?" I say. "I can't tell the difference."

The mother stands up quickly, the dummy sliding from her lap. "I'm sorry," I say. "I didn't mean to hurt your feelings, really." She looks hurt, and I feel strangely good about that and at the same time bad about feeling that way. And while I'm feeling those things, I'm apologizing, lamenting my horrible sense of humor and too-quick tongue, telling her what a good opportunity this is and how I'll come and see her, how I'll be her first customer, how very excited I truly am about having a fair in town, especially with a revival going on at the same time, things are certainly picking up aren't they, before we know it the state will give us an exit on the interstate.

She doesn't trust my apology for a minute, but pretends that she does and goes inside looking for Melissa. I'm even angrier with her since I had to apologize without meaning it, and I want to yell at her, "How come you're so fat and Melissa's so skinny?" but I don't. I sit on the swing as though it's a stationary chair, trying to be fair, wondering if I really want the mother to seek her own lowest point of misery in the daughter and stay there, deciding that I do.

The next evening Melissa stays in her room dusting cupids, and for the first time I notice the grace in her movements, the fragility. The mother runs from one room to the next, leaving a cloud of perfume wherever she stays for more than two seconds, forgetting her anger with me as she asks me to zip her shiny blouse, comb the back of her hair. She "la la" and "mi mi's" around the house like a singer, running in and out of Melissa's room, practicing her voice. "I've really got it down now," and she says, *Ello, I'm Ilbur Ight* in a voice strained through her teeth and too-rigid lips. "Dynamite," I say, "just terrific. You'll really wow 'em."

Around six o'clock things crank up—the revival preacher starts preaching with a larger amplifier. I look out the window and see a gospel rock band setting up in the tent; the preacher means business. The air smells like corn dogs, sweet grease, and a ferris wheel begins moving and so do some other indistinguishable rides, each with its own music to cover the disconcerting sound of metal on metal, at least ten different colors of neon. Both the revival and the fair are strung with thick black electric cords, no sign of where they're plugged in.

For a second I hope that we really will attract people, become some kind of annual sacred/secular event. But only a few handfuls come to the fair, another handful to the revival; people move back and forth between them. I leave my house and walk down the street, not to participate, just to look. The preacher works his crying people, is in the middle of a testimony, talking about himself. "I was egotistical," he says, "self-centered, until I discovered the Lord had a plan for me." I stand next to the tent, the moist green odor of a tent that's been used only recently for camping, listening to him tell me the story of his life which adds up to something about God helping him dodge paying rent in South America. "Nothing matters," he says. "Nothing that happens in the world as long as you yourself are saved."

The gospel rock band starts playing incredibly loud. I buy myself a Lemon Shake-It and watch the ferris wheel circle with no one on it and then with a small family on it and then a couple, the garish lights and the music. I look over to where the mother is sitting alone in her booth, surrounded by airplanes and no customers. But her eyes are thrilled as she eats a smoked sausage covered with green peppers and onions. She watches the rides, the lights. And back in town on their porches people sit and swing and cry and laugh, husbands touch wives, children show off, watching the end of the summer, knee deep in dust.

I go home, put a record on the record player. Melissa comes into the living room where I am sitting and takes a chair in the corner. She leans into the room, sits trembling, lips quivering. I should have guessed earlier, I think; the eyes are soulful, there is a life in there. The mother comes home, dumps her airplanes onto the sofa, telling Melissa what a success the fair was, what a great job she did. Melissa looks at her mother, looks out the window at the lights, tugs at the second sweater she's put on over the first one, her lip trembling more rapidly. "But they're leaving in the morning," the mother says. "They just found out they have to be in Illinois tomorrow night."

She begins a dance in the middle of the floor, an awkward, clumsy dance, her polyester jacket bouncing on her hips. Then the music stops and the lights go out in my house and, through the window, all up and down the street. It's dark and quiet where the fair was, the revival. "Too much electricity," Melissa says. "They've used up too much."

The mother picks up the airplanes in the dark, keeps dancing without music as she goes to Melissa and kisses the top of her head; the slick fabric of her jacket rubs the daughter's face. Sparks jump from Melissa's hair. I sink against a wall, touch a curtain, wonder why it has taken me so long to understand this, so simple, watch the mother waddle through the door. I am alone with the daughter sitting quietly in the chair. I feel a great sadness as I go to her and touch her hair where the mother has kissed her, feeling the room, the house, the town, the places we are all standing, slightly but definitely shake loose from the dust and begin to rise.